In Madison's Cave

In Madison's Cave

A Dialogue

Douglas Anderson

Frayed Edge Press
Philadelphia, PA

Published by Frayed Edge Press in 2021

Frayed Edge Press
PO Box 13465
Philadelphia, PA 19101

http://frayededgepress.com

Cover design by A.R. Melnik
Cover image by Thomas Sully
Portrait of Thomas Jefferson, begun 1821, finished 1830
oil on canvas
37.5 x 32.5 inches
American Philosophical Society. Gift of William Short, 1830.
Image courtesy of the American Philosophical Society

Publishers Cataloging-in-Publication Data

Names: Anderson, Douglas.
Title: In Madison's Cave / Douglas Anderson.
Description: Philadelphia, PA : Frayed Edge Press, 2021. | Summary: Fictional dialogue between two founding fathers explores the meanings behind Jefferson's Notes on the State of Virginia.
Identifiers: LCCN 2021935645 | ISBN 9781642510317 (pbk.) | ISBN 9781642510324 (ebook)
Subjects: LCSH: Jefferson, Thomas, 1743-1826--Fiction. | Adams, John, 1735-1826--Fiction. | Jefferson, Thomas, 1743-1826. Notes on the State of Virginia. | Friendship--Fiction. | Virginia-- History -- 1775-1865--Fiction. | United States -- Politics and government -- 1775-1783 – Fiction. | BISAC: FICTION / Historical / Colonial America & Revolution. | FICTION Literary. | FICTION / Political.
Classification: LCC PS3601.N334 I5 2021| DDC 813 A53--dc23
LC record available at https://lccn.loc.gov/2021935645

Indeed, I tremble for my country when I reflect that God is just: that his justice cannot sleep forever. . . .

Query XVIII, Notes on the State of Virginia

Advertisement

The following pages are the record of a disembodied conversation between two distinguished figures from the past who will introduce themselves soon enough. Rather, one of them will. The identity of the other will emerge in due course. The first speaker is eighty years old when the conversation begins. The second is eighty-eight. They have known each other nearly fifty years.

The chapters loosely mimic the design of a book that the younger man published long ago, beginning with an advertisement much like this one and ending with a series of appendices. The book has caused more than its share of scandals, though for many reasons it is unreadable. In places it is unbearable to read. To say any more would be to lapse into pedantry.

A handful of more obscure individuals whom the speakers mention are simple to look up, as are the text of a speech that the two men discuss and a large, engraved map that they study. Readers only vaguely familiar with the story of Samson might want to revisit the Book of Judges. The "Madison" of the title is an anonymous farmer who discovered a rich source of fertilizer in a modest limestone cave nearly three centuries ago and named it for himself.

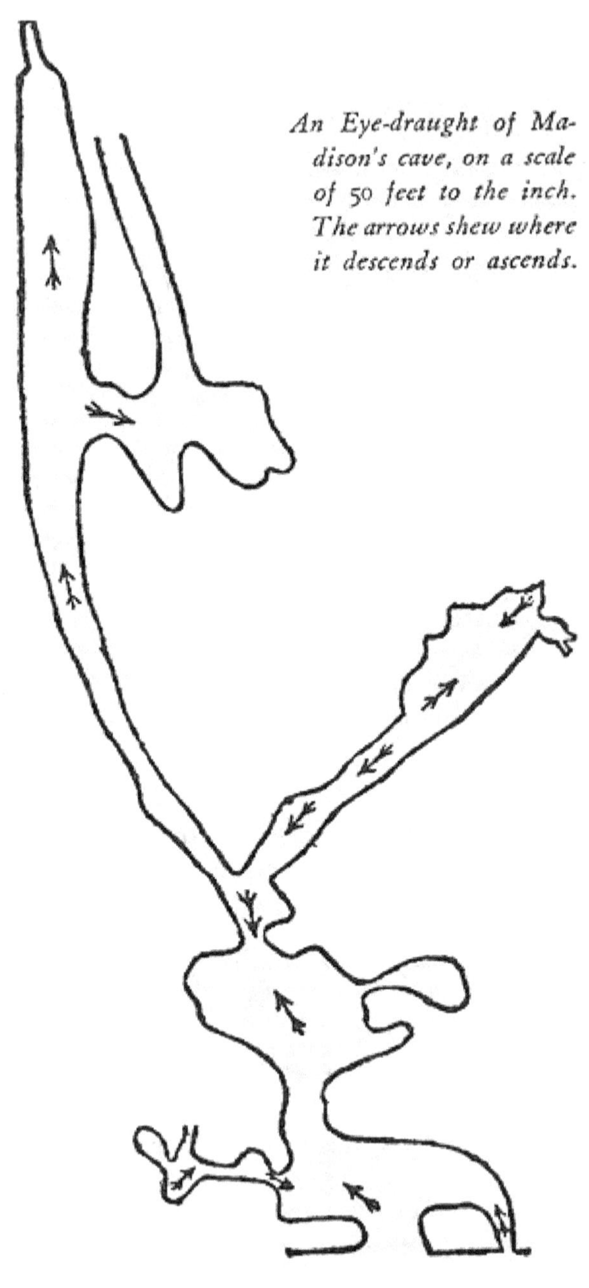

An Eye-draught of Madison's cave, on a scale of 50 feet to the inch. The arrows shew where it descends or ascends.

Limits

THE SOULS OF MEN ARE DEMONS, Apuleius once wrote, and though he was probably thinking of that old Greek obscurity the *daimon*, I rather prefer the blunter term, the bludgeon to the lyre. Daimons could come in different forms: the good from above, the wicked from below; some blessed, some cursed, and some provocatively mixed. The last category comes as a bit of a surprise, I suspect, an untidy confusion that throws our moral drama into a terrible disarray from which two thousand years of priests and poets have been unable to release it. Perhaps this stubborn, unruly streak explains my attraction to the *manes*, as the Romans called them—dwellers in shadow crossed by vivid strips of light or dwellers in light broken by deep bands of shadow, the maddening spiritual mixtures. I have been thinking a great deal about my own *manes* lately, my invisible but palpable demon.

More than once I have felt its presence, a faint thermal surge on an otherwise cool but perfectly still spring day—a sensation not conveyed by a passing breeze, for no breeze brings it and none disperses it. For two or three seconds at most, as I am walking in the garden or down a city street, I feel enclosed and then released, as if the plasma of a fine flame were briefly bathing my torso, enveloping my face. And then as suddenly as it comes, it goes. Does it have dimensions? So it would seem, since I am walking through it. But what if it is walking with me? How high does it reach? To the top of my head at least, but how much higher who can say? Even if I should happen to have a thermometer handy—and between you and me no sensible person is ever without a first-rate thermometer—I couldn't hope to measure the temperature change, to give a number to the fleeting experience.

Sometimes I think it might be worth my while to design a special vest or coat with pockets inside and out that could hold six or seven useful little instruments. Barometers, chronometers, miniature pendulums and spirit levels, devices for measuring wind and humidity, pulse and respiration, all primed to register their findings the instant that I step out of the house to cross the lawn. But then a little cloud of clerks would have to hover about, picking my pockets every few seconds to take down the information that my instruments supplied. Reverie would be out of the question. No self-respecting *manes* would bother to pay me a visit under such ludicrous conditions. And what would all these numbers be likely to tell me? That once I have taken ten steps from my porch I am not the same person I was when I shut the door? But I already know that. I already know that streams do not flow backward.

The numbers that matter tell me that I am an old man, that it is now forty years since I was forty and went into the cave to find out for myself whether the pathway up and the pathway down were really one and the same. But I don't mean to revisit that scene just yet. The cave is, at best, the second of the four pictures I plan to send you. Or perhaps the third. The order makes a difference, I suppose, but by the time that I am done presenting them, I hope you will see that they are all the same picture in the end. The modes of drawing vary. Certainly the quality is erratic. The most solemn and most personal of the four is little more than a marginal sketch. The others, at first glance, are simply maps; but you and I can probably agree that a map is always a picture, if the map-reader has any imagination whatsoever. One of the four is clearly more polished than the others, it being the one that I inherited rather than the three that I made myself, a public document of considerable scope and prestige—a surveyor's masterpiece, but as such no more than a masterful treatment of surfaces. I have updated it over the years as names and boundaries changed, as towns sprang up to fill in some of the blank spaces. At one point I had it engraved, as you know, but no sooner was the engraver finished than it was out of date once more. Heraclitus would have been amused.

You once wrote me that we two ought not to die before we had explained ourselves to one another. These little drawings are my explanation.

Now that I am reviewing all four of them in my mind, perhaps I should distinguish more carefully between their outward and their inward ambitions. The first is largely a matter of costumes, by which I mean the whole decorative exterior of the natural world, as well as our own exterior ornamentation from the skin on out. We live in an age of costumes, I know, but what age hasn't sought to cover its nakedness with its vanity? Even togas and tunics, simple as they were, strove to throw a cloak of rural innocence over the depraved aristocracy of the ancient world. At least our own pigments, wigs, and powders, lace ruffles, buckles, and crisp silk are at worst a childish vulgarity, even if the appetites beneath all the theatrical plunder are largely unchanged. It is an odd paradox when one thinks about it, since appetites are by definition ephemeral, little bodily storms that spring up and blow over. But there is an eye within each of them, I believe—a calm center where the whirling stops. For years I thought I could capture that calm in brick and stone, make it durable, fashion a secure dwelling amid the flux, or above it perhaps. Now paper and pencil will have to do.

These ramblings will make better sense once the pictures themselves are in your hands. You complain to me about the weakness of your eyes and the quiveration of your fingers, but the quiveration of the brain is more disabling than either. Many days now, on the threshold of my ninth decade, I find that I cannot draw a straight line from one subject to another, from one thought or one task to the next. Some of my distractions have subterranean origins—or subcutanean, I should say: a shifting of urgent interior tides. If my tutors and teachers had once explained to me the golden ratio between an active mind and an empty bladder, I would have devoted my life's energies to devising a painless and effective catheter. Opening a clear channel of navigation in some rocky, back-country stream is child's play by comparison. Long before any of us have the decency to turn into dust, we are just squalid sewer systems sluggishly coiling beneath palaces and parliaments, tenements and salons. A fleshly Venice, in fact, gaudy barges atop a pool of waste.

As I re-read those last few words, I am forced to admit that I have the makings of a hot preacher in me after all.

ꙮ

My first drawing, as you will soon see, is a much cooler effort. Indeed, other than you, no one will see it until after my death. Quite soon after, I hope, for I have set it in a drawer by my bedside, folded around some keepsakes of my marriage that should guarantee it careful scrutiny by my heirs, though by itself it is quite a modest little scrap, easily overlooked. Some grieving busy-body or another is sure to rummage through that drawer within an hour or two of my final exhalation, even as my *manes* and I are hovering on a nearby windowsill preparing to launch ourselves into the aether like one of Montgolfier's balloons. "Here, look here," an inquisitive grandchild will exclaim. "He has designed his grave marker. He has saved us a world of worry."

I will, of course, have done nothing of the kind. Cooler heads will eventually point out that the instructions are undated and unsigned. "But surely that is his hand," others will reply, "still recognizable if a bit brittle with an old man's quiverations. And the *I* and the *my* can only mean him. How else would you explain the name on the faces of the stone?"

"So much is clear, I agree. But why do you suppose he adopts such a brusque tone? Only these few lines, he insists, *and not a word more*. Dust he may well have become, but he is rather particular dust, if you ask me. Does he expect us to scribble a rat's nest of hieroglyphs up and down the obelisk, enumerating his triumphs? Is it really necessary to scold us from beyond the grave? He was no warrior pharaoh, to be sure, but he might have added one or two considerable distinctions to this modest list, don't you think?"

"He hated displays. You could barely get him to dress for dinner when guests were expected. Old friends and neighbors make allowances, but receiving a delegation of prominent strangers in a pair of worn slippers and an old dressing gown was an embarrassing affectation."

"Maybe this marker is another. Perhaps we shouldn't take these instructions seriously. They aren't in his will, after all."

"He hated wills too."

"But he made one."

I could go on in this dramatic vein, but I suspect the little fiction would quickly lose interest. My surviving relatives have chores to attend to, meals to arrange, well-wishers to receive, funeral arrangements to deal with, letters to write, legacies to distribute, and debts to pay or not to pay, as the case may be. I have left my affairs in a terrible state—a great deal of fuss lies ahead. The little scrap of paper that I have copied out for you won't trouble them for long amid the flood of other worries that await. A pity, since it is really quite a tidy little memoir, a talisman or a ghostly presence that, given time, might conjure up an entire cast of mind. One might even consider it several pictures in one. Three at the very least, a miniature portfolio on its own, depending on how subtle the conjuration that my heirs perform. I'll give you an instance or two of what I mean, though if your eyes were as unclouded today as those razor-sharp instruments of half a century ago, you would hardly need any assistance to penetrate the design.

Ask the budding scholar who takes your dictation to begin with the little preamble to the right of the gravestone sketch and read straight through the entire memorandum aloud, slowly and clearly, to a pair of final requests concerning materials and dates. I have included a brief inscription in quotation marks that I mean for my family to follow. The marks are so small that you probably won't be able to see them, however earnestly you might squint, and I don't expect even the most scrupulous secretary to give some vocal signal of their presence. They are there solely to lend an authoritative aura to my instructions. A few squiggles on the sketch suggest how the lines might appear on the obelisk, but I am not very concerned about the precise arrangement of the words.

Or should I say that my lack of concern is the essence of their arrangement? Indifference. A lovely word. Isn't that what the squiggles would convey to a practiced eye? A purposeful quiveration. I hope you can make them out with a small reading lens. I have done my best to duplicate the squiggles exactly as they appear in the original drawing. In any event, your amanuensis can describe them for you. Once the obelisk is actually put in place, the little scrap of paper will probably disappear, and with it this sly hint of my fondness for democratic affectation. My daughter and her husband will no doubt confer with the stonecutter and introduce a flourish or two, larger or smaller letters, an ornate capital here and there, perhaps an italic slant to add variety. Yet another instance of our primitive affinity for costumes.

Does your accomplished young secretary read Greek? I forgot to inquire. If not, then the ancient homily that I have set down for my heirs to consider may need to wait until your son's next visit. The two of you will immediately appreciate the confusion that I have introduced over my epitaph. In effect the little memorandum provides two, though I doubt if any of those gathered at my bedside will notice the odd conundrum. More and more, I find, we have begun to label our graves as if they were shipping crates, providing an invoice of their contents for a customs officer to assess. As an acknowledgement of inevitable forgetfulness among the living, the practice has a certain commonsense appeal. No one loves a well-laden and clearly labeled shipping crate more than I.

Rather than entrust my own labeling to another, however, I have written out one for myself in an effort to limit any egregious expressions of family pride or political preening. That is what my surviving relations and close friends will conclude as they confer over the contents of my bedside drawer. But any student of epitaphs will immediately recognize that the two brief lines of

Greek preceding the shipping label are, in fact, the mystic breath of the dead, precisely the kind of message that an emancipated spirit might choose to leave behind. What the living choose to do with the lines is another matter. The memorandum disavows "any interest in Monuments or other remembrances when, as Anacreon says,

> Ολίγη δε κείςομεςθα
> Κονίς, οςτεων λνθενΐων

But then, by way of remembrance, it promptly provides a gratifying inscription for a monument that it professes to scorn. I have made a career of such verbal feints.

Connoisseurs of graveyard verse are far rarer among my neighbors than among yours, but I can think of one or two who are likely to climb my mountain to pay their last respects before the commemorative scrap of paper is mislaid. They will certainly understand how to weigh my little preamble, though I suspect that they will be far too circumspect to interfere in a family matter. "Good for them," I can imagine you grumbling, "but why not provide a translation, if the homily is such a delicate expression of your ghostly sentiments? It would be a courtesy to those whose command of ancient tongues is not what it used to be." Or who never gave the ancient languages much thought in the first place, I might add. Why not two translations, in fact—one in Latin and another in French—enough to make up a Champollion stone that would allow any reasonably well-educated English reader to piece together my meaning?

I thought of doing so, but my *manes* convinced me that such a gesture would amount to an unwarranted accommodation just at the point, in our little memorandum, where the two of us have declared ourselves uninterested in courting our readers. We feel even less interest in the educational deficiencies of the general population than we do in monuments, but taunting people with their ignorance is both uncivil and pointless. Once one has descended into the dust, disappointment and gratification become meaningless vestiges of a former existence. It won't take my clever daughter long to trace the Greek quotation. She knows where I keep my commonplace book and can easily match up the characters with their source in those pages, even if she cannot read them. A few steps will take her to the shelf in my library where she can find the translator's original rendering:

A scanty dust to feed the wind
Is all the trace we leave behind.

"Aha!" she will probably exclaim, with a flash of her mother's mischievous nature. "It isn't by Anacreon at all but by some unknown pupil or wishful follower, one of the Anacreontic brood whose names have been lost forever!" If she mutters these triumphant words out loud and listens to herself, after a moment or two of thoughtful silence, she may begin to feel yet another invisible plasma tide flow warmly over her face and hands as she takes up the little scrap of paper once more and looks again over the opening words.

Whose spiritual essence will this new visitor be? Her mother's spotless *eudaimon* would undoubtedly delight in the rueful metamorphosis of an Epicurean into a Stoic, but the purest spirits never leave their celestial haunts to mingle in earthly matters. My *manes*, however, would have scarcely left its ravaged host behind when my daughter visits her father's library to decipher his curious note. No one will notice her brief absence. I have already been boxed up in my shipping crate and moved to one of the public rooms of the house in preparation for what I trust will be a very short and very simple farewell ceremony. No one is lingering behind but she. "The name is lost. Of course!" my daughter will say to herself. "He has set a little trap, left a last breadcrumb trail for me to follow, a last lesson to take to heart." I can't begin to tell you, old friend, the pleasure that this entirely imaginary scene has brought me as I jot it down. "We are a scanty dust indeed," my daughter will whisper at last. "We leave no names."

ꕤ

I did, though, leave a name to accompany the obelisk's inscription, if only to satisfy convention. My metaphysical scruples are not so profound as to require my surviving family to countenance a notorious ancestor scoffing at those who had gone to considerable trouble to visit his out-of-the-way tomb.

> "So I see. A sensible decision. You could hardly expect your grieving child to settle for an obscure snippet of ancient Greek on your gravestone, with or without a translation. But the shipping label itself is more than a little eccentric, if you don't mind my saying so. I had to ask my secretary to read it over twice before I was satisfied that he hadn't missed a line or two."

How good of you to notice! I expected as much. You were always a careful listener—thanks to your courtroom years, perhaps? Obscure or not, the Greek remains a useful counterpoint to the sort of postmortem theatrics that characterize even an eccentric shipping label. Indeed, the most eccentric labels are invariably the most theatrical, as my own may well prove to be by the time we are finished considering it. The Greek characters in my memorandum are able thespians, by the way. In certain moods they strike me as a tiny ensemble of performers, a jumble of dancing sticks or acrobatic bones, especially so if you consider that most of the pilgrims likely to pay a visit to my grave will possess little Latin and less Greek. No Greek at all would be better still. Once the ancient characters acquire names and sounds, weaving themselves into meter and making sense, we forget that they are things before they are symbols, a thicket of twigs and branchlets, stripped bare by a winter storm, or a skeleton slowly disarticulating itself as softer tissues wither away.

But as you say, the Greek won't be on the stone at all, unless my daughter decides to take matters into her own hands and places it there. She is certainly capable of doing so. "Not a word more my foot," I hear her say. "Not another English word perhaps.

What is the point of taking pains to transcribe those characters in two tidy parallel lines if he didn't intend to mirror his obelisk's inscription and invite the stonecutter to do the same? Why play a clever quotation game with me if he didn't mean something by it?"
I do, in fact, mean something by it, though I suspect I have been too clever or too obscure for my own good. It would not be the first time.

Pinckney used to tell me strange anecdotes about the ability of one of his people to read bones. "I have an old woman at home," he said, "who answers any question you might care to pose about the future. She keeps a beautifully woven cup of varicolored reeds filled with the most delicate bones you can imagine from any sort of dead creature she happens to find. The spinal segments of a snake's tail no bigger than your fingernail, the wing bones of small birds and bats, the skull of a vole, the tiny pelvic loop of an unborn kitten. I can't imagine where she finds them, but the mix has a mystery to it that she keeps very close. Apparently, some bones are more sensitive than others, more in tune with good fortune or with bad, with male clients or with female ones."

"For all I know," he added, "she keeps different little cups for different kinds of questions. A young man might turn up to consult her on the prospects of a love affair. New mothers might want to ask the bones about the fate of a sick child. An old man might wish to learn how soon he could expect to die. As you can imagine she does a booming trade in the quarter and for many miles around."

She would jostle the cup in her withered fingers, Pinckney said, mutter some kind of incantation, and dump the contents out on a smooth patch of ground. They must have fallen into a sentence, I suppose, for according to Pinckney she would gaze at them for a bit and then read out the message that the bones had spelled. No sooner had she finished but quick as a flash she would scoop her boney counsellors back into the cup and the moment of divination would be over. The spirits are not given to much elaboration and seem to have an aversion to prolonged inspection. We could learn some useful lessons from them. Those old sea-lords the Norsemen read bones. So did some Cherokee shamans in my father's time. Why shouldn't ancient Greek be descended from bones as well? Divination was dear to their hearts.

Where on earth can these reflections be leading? I set out to present you with the first of my four pictures and here I am musing about clairvoyant bones. Back to business then.

The first portion of my grave marker has a precise geometric nature, a "plain die or cube" the memorandum says, three feet on a side with no mouldings whatever to detract from its Euclidean purity. I have every expectation that this object will be troublesome to procure. Stonecutters can be a truculent breed. "You can't mean it, Mrs. R! A block where a simple slab will do? Such a waste. Did your father perhaps confuse this item with a cornerstone? It is certainly massive enough for that purpose, and you of all people know how cornerstones had vexed him of late. I don't suppose he wanted us to pull it up the mountain by hand?" My daughter's patience has its limits. "A cube he asked for and a cube he will have." But she may be all the more likely to ask herself, *Why even call it a die? Why free of mouldings?* Why, indeed?

Were she better versed in games of chance she would realize that only a cube with perfectly straight edges can be an honest broker of the fates. A little moulding here or there will bias the throw. One can cast lots with a die as readily as with a cup of old bones, though the die must be as regular in shape as it is possible to make it, and the faces must be numbered or marked to allow each throw to count. I have asked that at least three of the four visible faces of mine remain perfectly smooth, allowing only for the dates of my birth and my death to appear on the surface of the fourth. Most throws cast with such an object would yield nothing at all, enigmatic blanks with an occasional flicker of significance when the limits of my physical being happened to land face up on the felt of the gaming table. *Alea iacta est,* to be sure, but no one would be able to interpret the die's message after it falls.

Now consider the four faces of the obelisk above, a tapered shaft of coarse stone almost precisely my own height—not taken in the full bloom of manhood, I hasten to add, but the measure of my crumbling years, when the spine telescopes against itself and the shoulders stoop. Time has diminished me by a good two inches at least, I should say, judging from where the hem of my disreputable old dressing gown now falls against my leg. A trapezoidal shaft, then, an abstract statue, stripped of its limbs and with four faces rather than one, each face repeating the same words to any curious travelers who happen to stop by these remote crossroads:

Here was buried
Thomas Jefferson
Author of the Declaration of American Independence
of the Statute of Virginia for religious freedom
& Father of the University of Virginia.

That is how the unsigned bedside memorandum reads. And though my *manes* is indeed very particular about many things, it has not bothered to explain every detail of the inscription or why these words should be so much more gratifying than many others.

At one time a particular individual was, indeed, buried here but you must not expect that individual's physical remains to rest quietly beneath this stone, dipped in honey and wrapped in fine linen, with his desiccated organs stored in nearby canopic jars. He was buried here but he does not lie here. I have indeed tried to father a university, but in recent years I have despaired of ever founding one, as our legislators repeatedly quailed at the expense. Religious freedom is well worth enshrining in law, but strictly considered, the expression is not a proper noun and ought to have no more stature in the title of the statute than the prepositions "of" and "for." My daughter will probably opt for upper case letters, making a fetish of our principles.

Perhaps this latter feature of the inscription is only my private crotchet, but surely the modifier "American" in the third line is a political gaffe at the very least. And why stubbornly repeat the same words four times, once on each face of the stone? The Theban sphinx would pose a single question and then devour any traveler who could not answer. My obelisk offers three identical answers to all four points of the compass and waits for questions.

In any event, as you can see, the bedside memorandum refuses to provide much help, beyond adding a few perfunctory instructions. Make the monument of the same coarse stone that I used for the columns of my house in order to avoid tempting speculators in marble. Send my bust and pedestal down the mountain to the caretakers of my infant university, provided they agree to house those objects in the dome room of the Rotunda, surrounded by books. Carve the necessary dates upon the die.

These at least are steps that might be taken. I have pronounced no curse on any well-meaning descendants who may decide to thwart my wishes. An obelisk six feet tall is an extravagance, and my love of extravagance has already subjected my family to quite enough embarrassment as it is. My imaginary stonecutter is quite right. A simple slab would suffice. The still-born university at the foot of my mountain is suffering more acutely from a shortage of cornerstones than from a lack of marble busts. It is welcome to my three-foot cube if the Board of Visitors can see their way to finishing another building or two—the anatomical theater, perhaps? I would donate my body to be among the first dissections if I thought my daughter would stand for it. At the very least my bones might be properly prepared to hang in some convenient niche where the students might gaze at my remains as they pass; but then the inscription would need to be adjusted accordingly. "Here hangs the skeleton of Thomas Jefferson, like a gibbeted pirate or a rebel slave, his earthly frame picked clean by birds and flies."

You perceive, old friend, that my imagination has taken a ghoulish turn of late, like my spiritual brother, the Spanish painter who was compelled to hide his etchings of hags and bats from the officers of the Church. Pinckney told me the story in one of the first letters that he sent after presenting his credentials in Madrid. *Los Caprichos* the etchings were called, the whimsies or the flights of an uneasy mind. The memorandum I have sent you, and indeed this letter itself, are certainly whimsies of my own, though the Inquisition would find my little drawing quite harmless. Superfluous, in fact. A cube and an obelisk are perfectly familiar shapes. My description could hardly be misunderstood. Why bother with a sketch at all?

Because any stone must first be a thing before it becomes a symbol, my *manes* will reply. First surfaces, then depths, though whether the depths are worth exploring only you will be able to decide.

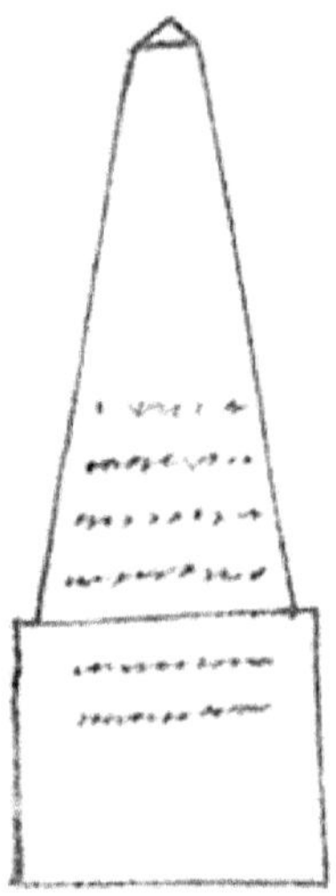

Navigation

> "What am I to do with these maddening breadcrumb trails? At least your daughter might expect to arrive eventually at a solution to her Greek riddle with the help of your commonplace book. But your letter leaves me with a tangle of things and symbols, blunders and bones, last wishes and ghoulish whimsies. Whoever happens to be buried in a grave generally remains there, it seems to me, with or without canopic jars. A founder you certainly are, however miserably your university may be foundering. As for the American declaration, surely that is little more than an opportunity for an enterprising stonecutter to run up your daughter's bill. If the rest of your picture collection proves as confusing as this first image, I must prepare my old head for a good scratching."

I QUITE AGREE. Too many riddles. Take the cubic die business for instance. One needn't be much of a craftsman with a chisel or a stone saw to recognize that shaping a block of rough granite into a perfect cube is by no means a simple job. The elegance of the obelisk may well delight the eye, but its sturdy base calls for an equally exacting set of skills, lest the delicately tapered shaft with its curious inscriptions take a tumble. The first embraces mass and density. The second tries to deny both. The cube is blunt matter. The obelisk wears a costume, though in saying so I seem to have slipped into another riddle.

I have just this moment returned from my forest retreat to find your latest letter waiting for me beneath a bushel of otherwise tedious correspondence. The hand of your secretary is as familiar to me as my own. The mere sight of the envelope restored my spirits. Ninety miles of hard riding over our crude western roads is more than an eighty-year-old man should attempt. Common sense tells me that I have probably paid my last visit to the little refuge that has given me such pleasure in my retirement. Its design too, I might add, begins with a cube, not of granite but of timber and brick, twenty feet on a side, centered within an octagon and surrounded by a ring of four slender rooms for sleeping or reading between the cube and the exterior walls. The ring rooms are octagons as well, though at a glance they seem to be elongated ovals. The cube itself is for dining. A narrow rectangular skylight bisects its ceiling, admitting eccentric bands of light as the hours and the seasons pass.

"The man wants a wizard's hideaway," some of my workmen probably mused as the interior spaces took shape. Others just set the building plan down to an infatuation with odd angles. "After all, he is a jumble of corners and angles himself, forking every which way like a bundle of sticks balancing on a saddle as he hunches over his drawings. Let him have his little necklace of octagons, if he fancies it."

In the end I could have my way in the forest, since I no longer had to allow for sheltering children and servants overhead, concealed by an inverted Palladian bowl where they might indulge their squirrelish ways. Nor did I require a miscellany of parlors, music salons, exhibit halls, and what-not to accommodate visitors or display the various curiosities that travelers have deposited with me over the years. Two of my grand-daughters would sometimes join me in the wizard's hideaway for a few weeks, but they kept one another company and have long outgrown the squirrelish stage. Their presence didn't disrupt my occult charms, though I confess that I am well past the desire to brew up further storms to shipwreck old political opponents. In the forest I escape the public stage that my crumbling family home has become—the ceaseless flood of letters that require replies, the parade of obligatory guests, the overseeing of repairs and projects and people. Not long ago I was compelled to set all other tasks aside in order to pose several hours each day for the greater part of two weeks, wearing an immense winter coat, while a young Philadelphia painter sketched my visage and form for a full-length portrait that I hope never to see. It will hang in the military academy, I am told—another institution of which I am the putative father.

If I had two skeletons to bequeath, I would certainly send one of them there as an appropriate exhibit, either to incite or to terrify our would-be warriors. As it is they will have to content themselves with my thin gray locks and withered cheeks, nestled like a dried pippin in a collar of Russian sable. "You must pose in the Tsar's greatcoat," my talented young visitor insisted, in an ecstatic quiveration. He could hardly contain his delight.

It is only another costume after all. When I put it on I resemble a lumbering black bison of the Missouri plains.

On the whole I am relieved that I will never have to see the finished canvas. Even my ceremonial home is far too deeply immured in the hinterlands to allow for a whirlwind jaunt to Philadelphia or New York. You and I have reached an age of "never agains," some of which are a source of relief, even if many others are occasions of sorrow. It saddens me, for instance, when I reflect that I will never again entertain one or two close friends beneath my wizard's skylight in the woods. It is a dining chamber built for flights of thought, for directing the mind upward rather than outward—and certainly not downward toward the meager country fare a forest kitchen is able to provide. My carpenters weren't entirely wrong to sense some hermetic intent behind the design of the house, though as mysteries go, this one is more practical than most. A cube inside an octagon suffers from a shortage of windows. It was necessary to find a way of admitting daylight into the room and of allowing the soothing sounds of rain to inform guests of a change in the weather.

"But why not a true oculus then? Architecture is really your first love, after all. Why not a central, circular opening like the dome of Agrippa's Pantheon so the soothing rain could fall directly onto your forest-loving guests? Or perhaps a paneled cap like the jaunty peak of the Florentine baptistry? The baptistry is another octagon, after all, and though it conceals no central cube, it has a central font precisely in the spot where you have placed your philosopher's dining table. One might even say the priest dines there when he administers the sacrament. An altar of reason to displace the altar of Romish superstition. The comparison is irresistible. I should think a man as willing as you seem to be to play figurative games with his gravestone would be eager to seize the same opportunity for his wizard's lair."

The two figurative games are bound to differ, though, since one is set in a dwelling place for the living while the other is a house for the dead.

But I take your point. I am perfectly happy to explain certain oddities of my retreat though I am afraid that the account will amount to just another intolerable tangle. Judging from the descriptions I have read and the engravings I have inspected, the Florentine baptistry is indeed an octagon topped by an oculus in the form of a lantern that mimics the chapel beneath. But a lantern illuminates a dark street or warns mariners away from rocks. The baptistry ornament does neither, nor does it allow much light to reach the chapel floor. Its eight glass panes are vertical rather than horizontal, and like a lantern it has a lid. For all practical purposes it is merely an axis in a religious machine, a spindle around which the interior ceiling mosaics revolve their biblical scenes, edifying the cluster of believers below who are doubtless in need of something interesting to study while the baptismal rites unfold and the priest mutters his mystical incantations.

Have I mentioned, by the way, that my two forest privies are likewise octagons, each with a little lead cap sealing its roof? Perhaps you could suggest a suitable mosaic theme for their interior decoration. Something more modest than the Florentine designs, of course, but equally uplifting.

The Roman Pantheon's circular eye, I admit, intrigues me, if for no other reason than that it is open to the elements, an option I don't enjoy for my dining cube. Agrippa's interior panels seem never to have served as frames for religious legends. In all likelihood they held a lattice-work of gilded bronze or gold leaf, perhaps in the shape of stars, a dazzling imitation of celestial light so intense as to nearly blind the reverent throngs beneath when the Roman sun pierced the oculus with its rays. Any and all gods inhabiting every conceivable heaven might be said to glitter in that fabulous vision. Or so the architect must have hoped, until some marauding Gothic prince stripped the precious flakes of metal from the moulded masonry to finance a fresh raid or to decorate a female favorite.

My dining cube is meant to awaken more intangible appetites. Indeed, in designing it I had some hopes that the few guests who joined me there might feel a need for only the simplest foods in the most moderate amounts, something like the experience of a monastic refectory but without the monks. Unlike the architects of the baptistry or the Pantheon, I have left the room's interior as unadorned as one of your meeting houses—plain white all around, with the exception of a small marble entablature where the sides of the skylight rest and a bit of wainscoting one would hardly notice. The effect is as plain as my gravestone die. Light is very nearly the only ornament of the space, and at different seasons and different times of day it inscribes an ever-changing celestial story against the walls, varying its intensity moment by moment as the afternoon progresses or as clouds drift overhead, bent by the corners of the room into curious angles that wax or wane by the hour, concentrated into brilliant accents at the end of a milky shaft or diffused in a single luminous band that stretches across the center of the ceiling directly over the dining table. The frames around the skylight's glass panes often cast pale gray ladders against the smooth plaster walls.

At one point I considered trying to calibrate the movements of the band of light, converting the whole room into a sort of solar calendar, but I dismissed the idea as a genuinely annoying affectation. The skylight's rays are sufficiently captivating on their own. Their various transformations mirror the mutability of the talk that accompanies a leisurely meal, now idle and now crisply focused, sometimes pursuing debates as straight as an arrow's shaft, while at other times prone to unexpected shifts in direction to the delight or the exasperation of the talkers. Both responses invariably soften as the daylight fades and the conversation draws to an end. Remember that my forest house is a retreat and not a salon. A midday meal there may well extend into the very early evening, but when the sun sets the occupants of the cube will disperse to the libraries, small sitting rooms, and bed chambers just outside its walls.

This architectural digression, I suspect, has only added another collection of infuriating breadcrumbs to those that sparked your original complaint. The moment I set out to send you a series of pictures, a cascade of competing images for the private gallery began to suggest themselves to my fancy. As I confessed in my gravestone letter, I have become a caricature in my dotage, the addled draftsman who cannot follow his own straight edge from one subject to the next. In mourning my forest retreat, I seem to have rebuilt it in my mind, attributing subtleties to the design that I could never have envisioned twenty years ago when I was drawing its plans. In those days I could still manage a draftsman's tools well enough to indulge my geometrical proclivities by envisioning a many-chambered retirement shell surrounding its cubic pearl.

Until the building actually took shape, however, I had not realized how perfect a dwelling it was for my *manes* and myself, and how much delight the two of us would take in climbing its shadowy ladders together.

I neglected to mention that the cornice entablature beneath the skylight imitates some moulding in the Baths of Diocletian. I found the pattern in an old architectural manual that I shipped north some years ago, along with the rest of my library, to replace the losses inflicted by a visitation of Vandals. But when I copied the carvings, I modified the ancient decoration by adding ox skulls to its Vitruvian medallions. If I thought the plan at all feasible, as soon as death drew near, I would take a final westward ride to the salt licks beyond the Alleghenies and mix my own bones with the mammoth remains that litter the earth. The Greeks considered the garlanded *bucranium* a fitting tribute to their ox-loving gods, silken heifers sacrificed on some green altar by a cohort of mysterious priests, as certain young English poets tell us. My philosopher's dining chamber transmutes these Doric superstitions, much as the Popes summoned the great artists of their day to plant cathedrals atop Diocletian's heap of rubble.

> "We are never to be done with skulls and skeletons, I see. But we have once again departed from the subject at hand. Your gravestone memorandum, signed or not, still holds my attention. It was clearly no afterthought on your part. Even my feeble eyes can pick out one or two places on the page where you struck out one phrase or inserted another, refining the wording as you went. The Greek characters are so carefully inscribed that they bring to mind a schoolboy's scrupulous calligraphy. The epitaph is even arranged in the precise lines that the stonecutter is to follow, with or without italics and ornamental lettering."

Don't overlook my fussy insistence on the use of the Old Style calendar for my date of birth. The sheet is clearly ready for a formal signing ceremony. And yet I never signed it. My *manes* took the pen from my fingers.

What a great show we feeble creatures make of our signatures! Adding curious flourishes here and there, with fastidious cross-hatchings, florid under-scorings, and imposing capital letters that loom over our names like Corinthian porticos on the façade of a noble family home—present company excepted, of course. Your three concise syllables made an enviably compact statement on any document to which you applied them. Three sharp taps of a carpenter's hammer, as it were. Yet even after four decades, we both close our correspondence with a ceremonial bow: "I am as ever, sir, your humble and obedient servant," or "with assurances of my unvarying affection and respect, I am," or "I am, my dear sir, with Sincere Esteem your friend." Even when a simple *affectionately* or *yours sincerely* suffices, our full names always follow, as if each casual note were the Peace of Paris. Is the grip of custom so hard to break? Are we seeking to ingratiate ourselves with some surreptitious audience?

As long as we are on the subject of curious flourishes, why on earth does my epitaph lay claim to the Declaration of American Independence? The awkward adjective is entirely unnecessary unless I am envisioning a party of pilgrims a thousand years hence. Casual tourists from another heavenly body might also require a general hint or two about the import of the strange ruin before them. But the visitors I in fact have in mind are our immediate descendants, the very ones who will find the extraneous word especially puzzling.

"What in God's name were his family thinking when they placed this inscription on his grave? What other declaration could possibly be meant than the American one we celebrate each July with bonfires and whiskey? No one even uses the official title any longer, 'The Unanimous Declaration of the Thirteen United States' and so forth. Or is it 'A Declaration by the Representatives of the United States'? Who can keep such things straight! In the end it is simply 'The Declaration of Independence,' plain as day. Only a pedant would split hairs over the label."

Here was buried just such a pedant, a lifelong splitter of hairs. Moreover, this stubborn error appears on all four faces of the obelisk. What could possibly explain such obstinacy? Is it a lesser or a greater claim to have authored an American declaration, a unanimous declaration, or simply the Declaration? At the very least visitors will descend my mountain in a state of fruitful irritation, determined to look more closely into titles and texts when their faculties are not addled by holiday punch. They will depart as pedants in their own right.

❧

Unless I greatly misjudge your nature, you are about to voice a measure of skepticism. Were it not for the tremors in your fingers, you would be seizing a pencil at this very moment to scratch your objections in the margins of my letter.

"Indeed, I am. For one thing, you give your future pilgrims far too much credit. Most tourists are not inclined to brood so over the shrines that they visit. They are on a country jaunt, and your little mountain happens to lie conveniently close to a comfortable inn as they wend their way toward some of the medicinal springs into which you plunged your Fahrenheit's thermometer, so many years ago. They are in search of relief from a winter of rheumatic complaints. As long as they are in the neighborhood, they will gladly visit your grave, stopping at the public house on the way up the slope for a refreshing drink while they entertain one another with tales of your scandalous legacy."

You are probably right.

"I know I am right. Scandal and slander are the breath of life to our zealous fellow countrymen, as you and I have good cause to know. Not a day goes by that I fail to receive notice of another bold editor or aspiring politician who accuses me of whoring after kings and nobles, craving ribbons and titles, sacrificing the liberty of the Many on the reeking altar of the One. Your garlanded *bucranium* is a quaint indulgence compared to the atrocities in which I am said to delight, the dark stratagems that I once hatched in the councils of power, before I got my eyes put out and like a disgraced Oedipus crawled into exile. I forbear reminding you of the vices that have been laid to your own account. My neighbors need not look to Spain to feed their ghoulish imaginations. They consider you and your fellow planters to be denizens of a licentious inferno, just as Virginians have long trembled at Santo Domingo and as the island gentry, in turn, have gazed in mock horror at the mines of Brazil. On around the globe, for all I know, the cycle of prurience runs its great circle from pole to pole, a whirlwind of voyeurism and lust. I cannot share your confidence that a calm of sorts lies at the heart of the storm. The souls of men are demons indeed, through and through. I would not hold much hope that your magical gravestone will exorcise them."

Exorcism is a game for priests. I was thinking more of cautery when I crafted my provocative shipping label, or of opening and draining a vile pool of mental infection something like the interior pockets of pustulent matter that have set your imaginary rheumatics on the road to our sulphur springs. Let them rub their inflamed joints and tender abscesses, drink their ale, and mock my inscription all they like. At some point one or two in the group may grow ominously silent over a half-empty mug, sensing perhaps a discreet sneer in my reference to an "American" declaration, some wholly imaginary undercurrent of contempt that had not been quite so noticeable to the sober mind. Every tavern table that I have ever observed in my life has its happy drunks and its savage ones. I am counting on the savage drunks to cause a stir. Demons attacking demons, if you like, just as Dante dreamed.

"What did the man mean by that sly insinuation anyway? American declaration indeed! And in the very next line of his inscription he preens himself over Virginia's proclamation of religious freedom, as if freedom in the mouth of a Virginian were not bound to leave a foul taste. Who gave him and his snuff-sucking crew the say-so over what we can or cannot do with our meeting houses and parishes? What happens when some free-thinking, loose-living, athiestical Virginia dandy stumbles across the Potomac and spits on one of our Maryland bishops? Their Virginia freedom will look rather puny in one of our courts of law. We make statutes too, by God! See how you like the taste of religious freedom, Maryland style!"

Before long a serious row breaks out—a brawl perhaps. The tavern keeper strives to restore order to save his furniture and crockery, if nothing else, and summons the local constable to make arrests. In time the whole quarrel makes an appearance in the popular press, reprinted up and down the coast in those scandal-loving papers that you rightly despise, and that I have no good reason to defend, until their zeal for circulation and their love of controversy inadvertently startles the long-dormant public mind. Surprising transformations of the understanding do not always require colorful drunken outbursts to set them in motion. Perhaps a politician or an editor, on a brief tour of information, stops by my gravestone in search of a grievance to nurse or a story to tell. Such a traveler might vaguely recall how many bitter disagreements lay hidden in our spurious continental unanimity. How grudgingly some of those signatures seem to have affixed themselves to our American declaration, shuffling slowly forward at the weary end of a long July afternoon to grasp a reluctant pen, freshen its ink, and squeeze a scarcely legible endorsement onto a lower corner of the sheet.

"Maybe the bolder hands will be the first to hang," some of these grumblers may have hoped. Or the first to find themselves besieged by their irate neighbors at home once they realize how imprudently their representatives have shackled them to a band of slaveholders, or a conniving cabal of merchant bankers, or a troop of semi-savage frontier farmers and hunters not much more civilized than the scalping parties that prey on them. "For the time being I have swallowed my objections to this presumptuous document," the grumblers tell themselves, "but I will vomit them up at the first opportunity."

For my own purposes, I have kept the sadly wounded draft that I submitted to Congress, with all their deletions and changes carefully recorded. After my *manes* and I have fled, I count on my heirs to publish it so that curious pilgrims may be able to consult the words as they confront my obelisk. The various modifications are undoubtedly improvements, but they also amount to an Hogarthian progress of the passions in reverse, a little pageant of restraint hastily captured by a furtive voyeur lurking just outside a stuffy meeting room. The doors have been left ajar in the hope of drawing a breeze through the crowded chamber within, where a score or two of fervent speakers are agitating the sultry afternoon with their frantic fans and heated words. It is an electrical air. Even through a thin gap between the panels of the door, one can feel the impalpable fluid build toward a moment of crackling discharge, when the energies spend themselves and achieve a momentary equilibrium before the whole process repeats itself over the next contested clause.

Do we have inherent rights or do we only have certain ones, the nature of which we are only partly prepared to put into words? Do we mean utterly to expunge a poisonous social compact and begin the human community anew or do we intend only to tinker with the status quo? Have we brought to the bar of a candid world an unsullied character or a deeply polluted one? These questions loom like a bank of thunderheads over the preamble alone, but then I have ever found that preambles are the most perilous passages in any statute or petition. What sort of creatures are we, measured against the Milky Way and the nebulae? By what right do we address the powers of the earth and by implication the powers of the universe? Never mind your feverish list of petty colonial complaints. Present your credentials to the Supreme Court of the Cosmos. Do you have legal standing here?

> "Surely no one in that stifling little room imagined himself addressing an audience buried deep in the Milky Way or wrapped in some nebular cloud! We were envisioning at most a few truculent members of Parliament, a French foreign minister, a Dutch banker or two hoping for a successful speculation at the expense of his arrogant neighbors."

Then why invoke the course of human affairs? Why not invite those ministers, bankers, and petty politicians to a feast they are capable of appreciating? The amelioration of human destiny as a whole has limitless scope. When we were measuring our opening words, dynastic time did not much concern us. We did not confine our attention to the Christian Era only—or to the civilized legacies of Egypt, India, or the Persian crescent. No. The entire planetary panorama since Genesis lies behind my opening clause, a spectacle best seen from the orbit of the Moon, I should think. If our declaration pertained only to the fate of a particular cluster of settlements on a stretch of ragged Atlantic coastline, then the intrusive "American" in my shipping label would hardly seem worth a second thought. It would amount to no more than a tacit clarification of the document's limits: when in the course of American affairs and so on. No gravestone pilgrim would take notice.

"As I recall, we debated every *and, but, when,* and *wherefore* as those days wore on. To begin by writing *American affairs* would have been to state the obvious. Why bother? Franklin boiled the entire polishing process down to the challenge of a tradesman selling hats. Don't ask too much of the customer, he advised, and above all no long-winded lectures on workmanship. The main thing is to get as many people as possible to walk out of the shop with your merchandize on their heads. Or with your words inside their heads, as the case may be."

Precisely. He was trying to lift my spirits as the hacking and hewing went on. Shall we magnify our resentments or muffle them, and which posture is likely to be the most effective? It was not the kind of question even a savvy tradesman would have been likely to pose. Even after fifty years I find myself surprised at how carefully we listened to various versions of this or that phrase and imagined ourselves delivering the words before the audience of the ages, strutting and fretting, while just outside the windows of the meeting room we could hear squabbling children, fishmongers hawking their wares, the scape of the manure shovels on the pavement.

We consider ourselves thirteen independent "states" at one point and yet a single "people" at another. An understandable but disquieting ambivalence. The use of foreign mercenaries and Indian raiding parties against us ignites our righteous fury. "Barbarous and merciless," we cry, yet we prudently delete the references my draft makes to the slave uprisings that were among our deepest fears. Consider how much this excision exposes, how naked we suddenly become! We suffer, yes, but we also inflict suffering and are wary of the retribution we invite. We resist oppression and we oppress resistance. Creatures of shadow crossed by bands of light and creatures of light immured in shadow. Perhaps my drunken brawlers will arrive at the same realization when they sober up. We are at best a people who only mean to be free.

"Ah. I remember that last change quite clearly. Despite our reservations in the committee, we agreed to send your wording to the whole body. 'A people who mean to be free' you called us in the draft's closing sentences, but a 'free people' we became in the declaration's final version. The whole Revolution transpires within a single marginal emendation. That is no Hogarthian cartoon."

No. And I am certainly the last person to object to a change that intensifies the feeling that our words convey. I threw too much heart into portions of my draft, knowing full well that a roomful of seasoned heads would impose the necessary verbal restraints. But this is one imposition that troubles me still, more than all the other changes combined. Self-evident truths and inalienable rights are little more than slogans, when all is said and done. Important slogans, I agree, but all the more susceptible to manipulation. Roman emperors marched under the banner of the Senate and the People long after their senate had become moribund and the people a vile mob. Paris bloodied itself under the guise of equality and fraternity.

An ideal is both an aspiration and a mask. Life, liberty, and happiness are laudable aspirations, to be sure, but the first is seldom an unqualified good, as your weakened eyes and palsied fingers can tell you. At best it is simply the necessary corporeal condition without which the second two terms are moot. Liberty is scarcely a synonym for freedom. It merely enables us to realize or to betray our hopes. Happiness is as fleeting as it is intense. You and I once considered the uses of grief and concluded that it is a school of relinquishment, a stern instructor that seams the face and furrows the brow with the emblems of a bitter endurance. It gives weight to our words. Is happiness simply its precondition? Should I have written "life, liberty, and the pursuit of grief"?

I have acknowledged that I am a master at splitting hairs. I wish that any pilgrims or idle travelers who pass by my gravestone might brood over the language of my shipping label.

"And having brooded sufficiently, what then? What are these newly enlightened pilgrims hoping to achieve?"

The complete emancipation of human nature. Signs of the ripening process are no doubt far more evident to observers in the Milky Way than they are to us. Vast distances can soften history's jagged contours into a smoothly graduated curve. A ship will tack ten thousand times yet adhere to its invisible course and safely reach port. The complete emancipation of human nature is, I trust, our destined harbor, though I do not expect to live to see it.

"Nor do I, nor will any of our descendants, I would venture to predict. What good does it do to set up such unattainable goals?"

I have asked myself precisely that question for the last half century at least.

"What conclusion do you come to?"

That it makes life interesting. A trivial compensation, you might say, and four decades ago I might have agreed with you, having buried within the space of a handful of years a wife, two infant daughters, and a nameless son who lived only seventeen agonizing days. But I have been in the cave since then; in more than one cave, in fact, re-examining the conditions of my existence on each visit and comparing them to my unreachable ideal. The complete emancipation of human nature. Not happiness. Not freedom from suffering. Not freedom in any of its countless formulations. Perhaps I should have made it my gravestone inscription. Here was buried one who dreamed of the complete emancipation of human nature. My *manes*, I think, might approve of the change.

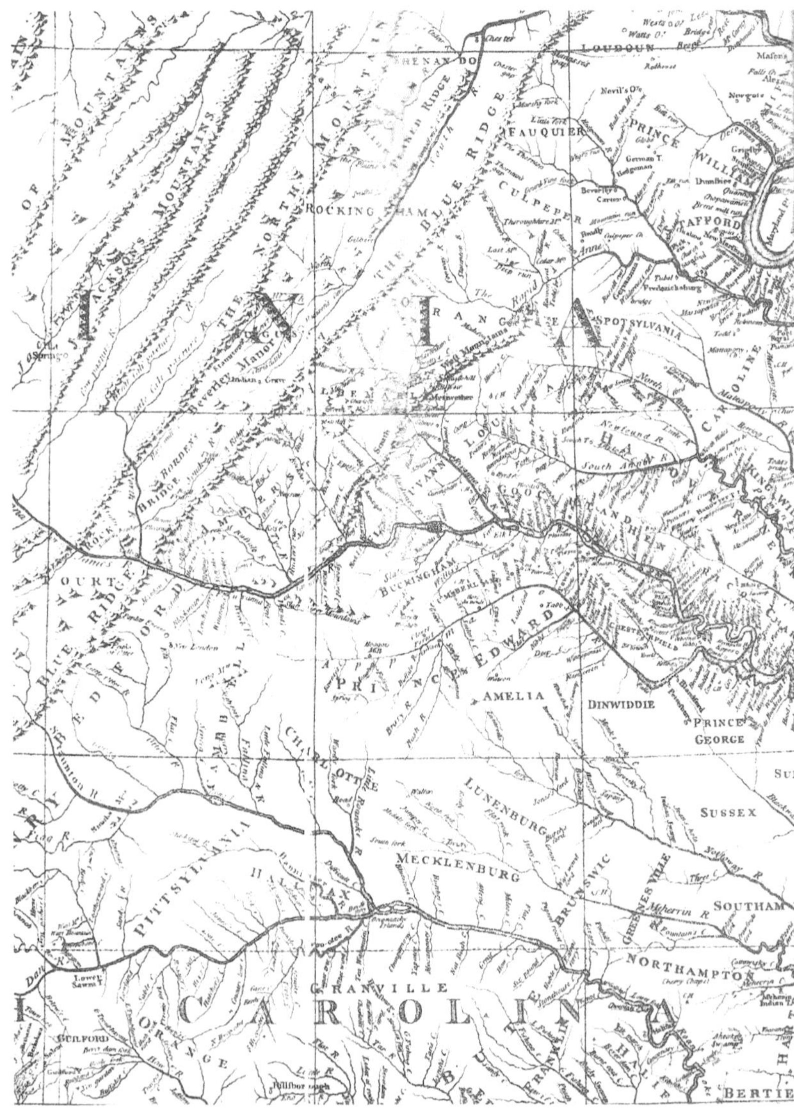

LOUDOUN
FAUQUIER
PRINCE WILLIAM
CULPEPER
ROCKINGHAM
THE BLUE RIDGE
JACKSONS MOUNTAINS
SPOTSYLVANIA
CAROLINE
BUCKINGHAM
EDWARD
AMELIA
DINWIDDIE
PRINCE GEORGE
SUSSEX
LUNENBURG
MECKLENBURG
PITTSYLVANIA
NORTHAMPTON
GRANVILLE
GUILFORD
CAROLINA
BERTIE

Rivers and Mountains

"You and your *manes* craft letters in the same spirit that you design obelisks, proposing answers that amount to questions in disguise. My young secretary has begun to dread their arrival, since reading them invariably provokes me into volleys of dictation.

"I have a flurry of fresh inquiries to pose that your margins would scarcely accommodate even if I were still capable of holding a pencil. Don't be alarmed if my replies should happen to arrive in bundles of three or four. I rattle off a few observations one day and affix my feeble signature to the page, but by the next morning I have thought of a hundred things to add and after rousing up the household I begin another letter, and the next day another, until one of my saucy grandchildren snatches the envelopes and sends them off to the post in a heap. No sooner is a batch gone, than I am in a fidget to hear from you again.

"Meanwhile, let me badger my long-suffering scribe with my latest round ofthoughts.

"Bequeathing your skeleton to one academy or another seems more whimsical than ghoulish. Clearly, my old friend, you have forgotten the blithe irreverence of the young. They are far more likely to whisk your skull away to a neighborhood tavern as a target for mock toasts and drinking songs than they are to Hamletize over the sad remnants of your fame. Mixing your bones with mammoths is more whimsical still, though to my mind consorting with ancient giants has a certain appeal. Even your formidable frame is likely to suffer by the contrast, but as your Anacreontic homily sagely notes, the contrast will dissipate with the dust. Why convert yourself into a relic at all, even in jest? Why, for that matter, consent to leave behind a formal portrait draped in the leather and fur of an eastern tyrant, unless you hope to be remembered as a Pawnee hunter wearing a prize trophy? These are frivolous gestures, I know, only one of which you have actually indulged. Compared to the legacies that your obelisk celebrates they are beneath notice. But a frivolous moment can be as revealing as an earnest one.

"Perhaps that curious truth explains your octagonal privies.

"As it happens, I do have a suggestion for their ceiling decoration that might appeal to you: seven stars in each of a suitable size, all cut from a mirror and arranged against the lead sheets on the underside of the roofs in a pair of simple constellations. Ursa Major in one privy and Ursa Minor in the other. The many advantages of the designs should be evident to anyone, beginning with their simplicity, their negligible cost, and their ease of installation. A privy is a chapel of ease after all. You might have a good woodcarver place great and little bears over the respective doors, a feature that your great-grandchildren would surely approve.

"The hopes that you entertain for your enchanted epitaph are far-fetched in the extreme. Most pilgrims will puzzle over your inscription for a minute or two and then dismiss it as a personal oddity roughly equivalent to an outdated fondness for reading Greek. What your words require is a party of wandering philosophers wearied by the excesses of Plato, Hume, or Rousseau and eager for a fresh conundrum to stimulate their wits. Your American declaration should suffice. Thunderclouds did indeed loom over us as we wrestled with your elegant draft. On the whole the electrical air did us good. But within a few weeks of affixing our signatures to the sheet, we began to disgorge our differences.

"How, for instance, should we apportion the financial responsibility for our mutual defense? A simple enough question, one would think. Does the labor of a slave enrich or deplete the public coffers? Should the southern states be taxed to reflect the strong arms and broad backs of those who will shoulder the burden of the war, black and white alike? *Only if your cattle count as people!* was the fiery reply. We had barely finished taking our marriage vows before beginning divorce proceedings. That instant marked the onset of a national brawl that no parallel of latitude running from the Dismal Swamp to the Pacific Ocean, no flimsy dividing line separating slave territories from free ones, is likely to resolve. The present Congress seems to believe that we can impose our consciences upon a landscape as easily as we plow a furrow or cut a block of coarse stone into a handsome trapezoid. But you and I both know that the landscape is just as likely to bend the conscience as the other way around.

"And then what to make of your faith in the emancipation of human nature? Does this aspiration come from the same pen that tells me the souls of men are demons? Would you emancipate such beings and allow them to unleash their inner turmoil on the world at large? Remember your tavern table with its happy drinkers and its savage ones. Is that not a picture in miniature of the emancipatory goal you envision?

"If I recall correctly you once explained to the readers of your *Notes* the dread you felt at the age-long accumulations of rage and fear seething beneath the surface of Virginia's placid valleys and misty ridges. I still have the volume on my shelves but do not trust my old eyes to find the place. Deep-seated prejudices and ten thousand recollections of great wrong had set the stage for a racial inferno, you wrote. Extermination was the inevitable outcome, a mutual war of slave against master in which the Deity must inevitably side with a victimized people. What cave could possibly provide a secret solace for this nightmare? A glittering deposit of some unknown salt or mineral that one of Pinckney's wise old women could distill into a curative elixir? Such a medicinal dose would lure even me from my rocky northern farm to take the healing waters at one of your southern springs. But I cannot believe it exists.

"The post beckons, and I have scarcely finished the overture to my remarks.

"I am, sir, as ever, your most affectionate and unchanging friend."

ꝏ

I AM DISMAYED AT THE HINT OF CONTEMPT that crept into my last letter as I mocked the dandified signatures of an old comrade or two, ridiculing in the same breath the professions of respect and friendship that fill our correspondence. It was a brittle satire that shatters on the rock of your affection. Such constancy alone gives me some hope that my faith in human nature is not misplaced, despite the evidence with which you delight to bombard me that our globe may well be the madhouse of the universe.

It has been some twenty years now since your wife and I took the first tentative steps toward resuming a steady exchange of mutual confidences between our households. She reminded me then of how painful the late political bitterness had been, how deeply the public invective had wounded her, how you and she had come to doubt my integrity and my friendship. Which of the two opposing political camps was the most venal, you once asked me, not long after we had resumed sending one another these letters, and offered your own answer in the blink of an eye: put them in a bag and shake them and see which pops out first. Together we shook the bag for a decade or more, and whenever we opened it, a different spitting feline emerged.

At the time I offered the whole tenor of my life as a counterweight to the stinging barbs that some newspaper porcupine or other had attributed to me or that I might well have hurled into a private letter that made its way to the press. We were, one and all, blown about by storms that made navigation almost impossible, some of our own making perhaps, but much of the onslaught was inflicted by jealous neighbors who despised our new-born institutions and gloried in our flaws. If I had thought to do so then, I would have suggested that the two of you consider me a beleaguered ship, struggling against powerful winds and high seas, trying to regain the compass bearing that had guided it through past dangers. Over the years, you and I did weather the tumult. We have at last taken a fresh sighting of the stars with such feeble instruments as remain to us.

I do, by the way, applaud your suggestion of placing the constellations in my octagonal privies. Though in the case of the privies, of course, the bears are interchangeable. One wouldn't wish to discourage Major from visiting Minor, or vice versa.

Addressing our outward weaknesses is one thing. The inward ones are far more intractable, far more crippling. Eastern tyrants may be dealt with in the age-old way, as Brutus dealt with Caesar, but such a remedy is doomed to be temporary, as the French have lately shown by shedding one arrogant imperial master only to fall victim, twice over, to another before closing the mad circle with a royal restoration conducted at the point of a gun. A complete transformation of human nature must be an irreversible one, an interior one, carried out individual by individual, a sea change that does not leave hidden reservoirs of lust or ambition or greed untouched.

Can such a metamorphosis be imposed from without? The preamble to our statute for religious freedom denies it, but you do as well when you denounce the folly of trying to inscribe our consciences on an impassive landscape. This Quixotic effort to turn an unmapped continent into mutually hostile quarantine zones is a precise equivalent to the laws of religious conformity that the Virginia act was meant, once and for all, to repudiate. Mental and spiritual conformity is a ridiculous delusion. The body can slip into any number of fashionable disguises, but the mind cannot be so easily transformed. It can be driven into hiding by its own fears or appetites. For a time, perhaps, it can be compelled to acknowledge the superficial demands of a state or a church. But it can only be purged of its vices or freed from the bondage of bigoted passions by the instruments of truth and reason, and they are cave dwellers by nature, inhabitants of the spirit's deepest recesses.

Patience, too, is part of the healing elixir—the most essential ingredient, I expect. Difficult cures are always incremental. The recovery is the longest where the disease is most severe, and it is often broken by periods of relapse, the struggle of an established sickness to maintain its frenzied claim. No spiritual plague is so severe as the one that currently disfigures my neighbors and myself, but the same infection breeds in the counting houses and mansions of great cities, north and south, on both sides of the ocean. Human vermin carry it from port to port.

How gratifying to learn that you have not forgotten my peculiar book!

A reader as voracious as yourself could be forgiven any lapses of memory, even where the work of old friends and colleagues might be concerned. To recall specific passages in detail, down to the odd turn of phrase, is beyond hoping, yet I find that your recollection is nearly perfect. My obelisk may yet be exerting its occult influence on your thoughts, even in its paper form. Imagine how potent its magic will be when the blocks are actually carved and set in place on the wooded slope where the graves of my family lie.

But a party of wandering philosophers such as you envision will almost certainly be puzzled to find no reference in my epitaph to any writing that I might have left behind, other than a bowdlerized broadside declaration and a single legislative act that is scarcely two pages long. "But what of that exhaustive treatise on his native state?" these learned pilgrims are bound to ask. "What of his *Notes on Virginia*?"

"All those painstaking tables of plants and animals, his meticulous temperature records and wind charts, the census of native tribes and their powerful confederacies he compiles! His invaluable critique of the state's constitution! He cannot have been indifferent to such a work. Why does his gravestone consign the book to oblivion?"

The question supplies its own answer. In appearing to forget the *Notes*, my shipping label in fact remembers them all the more vividly, just as in neglecting to sign my bedside memorandum, my *manes* and I have etched it into the minds of my heirs.

The act for establishing religious freedom, for instance, is one of the book's appendices. My gravestone has not forgotten the fact. Nor has it forgotten the scheme of public education that one of my chapters sketches out with ruthless economy. The obelisk will remind even the idlest pilgrim of my interest in establishing a university. It trains a mental telescope on the distant campus and, at the same time, on the pages of my sadly neglected *Notes*. I fully expect the last two lines of my shipping label to act as a subtle magnetic field, drawing the reader's thoughts in the direction of a curious volume that is at worst unbearably tedious and at best badly out of date.

To that end I have been busy scribbling corrections in the margins of my own copy over the years, pasting slips of paper into the binding to modify my wording, inserting a new page here or there to make more extensive changes and improvements. The process is not unlike maintaining a house. Even to my pedantic mind, however, these are all minor touches. The book as it stands is sufficient to the task that I originally envisioned for it.

"You mean, I take it, the task that the French envoy envisioned. He posed a handful of questions. You racked your brains and supplied the answers. No doubt there is more to it than that, but I do relish playing the dismissive skeptic."

I can see some clarification is overdue. When I was describing to you my forest retreat, you may recall that I disparaged a masterpiece of Renaissance architecture. The Florentine baptistry may well be a religious machine, but you and I can probably agree that it is exquisitely engineered to serve the needs of priestly ambition. "The whole world gazes," you once hissed in a fine fury as we contemplated its gilded doors and glittering mosaics. But it is no mean feat to capture the whole world's gaze.

In these letters of ours, in my gravestone memorandum, and in the four pictures that I have promised to send you, I am assembling a very different sort of machine, one designed to assist in the eventual realization of my improbable emancipatory ideal.

The pictures are at best schematic hints, a few pulleys and ropes salvaged from behind the scenery. All four are latent in the second of the series if one possesses a good reading glass and knows where to look. But a reading glass will only be necessary when we turn to the engraved map carefully folded into the back matter of my *Notes*. The volume as a whole is the finished mechanism and must be assembled, if at all, not between my covers but inside the reader's mind. The dream of complete emancipation is lodged in its pages, where I expect at least a few observant souls to stumble upon it once my obelisk has cast its spell. They will need good lanterns to find it.

My bedside memorandum and the gravestone it describes are only the first two breadcrumbs on what will prove to be a circuitous trail by the time I have finished describing it to you. The inscription on the obelisk will direct a certain number of sober pilgrims to the next set of signposts lodged in the vestibule of my book. Like its own species of cave, it has an opening to the light of day—an Advertisement I call it—where the explorer can briefly pause to collect his wits, ruffle the volume's pages, examine its table of contents, and decide whether or not to plunge into its depths.

I have sometimes claimed that the map carefully tucked away in the end papers is more valuable than the whole of the *Notes* that precede it. Very few readers will be deceived by such false modesty. I began writing partly as a distraction from the anxieties of governing my contentious fellow Virginians, but I finished the book to avoid killing myself.

Only my most intimate friends and relations would have known enough of my private circumstances at the time to recognize the nature of the wounds to which the Advertisement alludes.

"Surely he means the wounds of the Revolution," most later readers will assume. "The war was of course a terrible cataclysm, but he does not intend to aggravate old injuries. These pages are his peace offering."

A peace offering, they most certainly are not. I had scarcely begun work on the book when an enemy raid forced me to make a hasty flight from my home with a grieving wife who had buried our infant daughter not two months earlier. I bundled her into a carriage with our two surviving girls, pursued by the spite of my political opponents as much as by Tarleton's cavalry. Weeks later a return journey across miles of rugged trails under a cloud of discouragement and disgrace crippled my wife's already weakened constitution and contributed to her death the following autumn, a few months after giving birth to our last child. One can trace our route on the map my *Notes* include, but why would anyone think to look for it? To run my finger over the engraving is to touch the livid welts of an angry scar.

Just as the vestibule of a cave can convey echoes from its depths, so my Advertisement hints at the subterranean channels ahead.

What provocative murmurs might my neighbors hear in the restrained apology I offer for my book's many imperfections? What species of old wounds will occur to them? Not a few of them employ specialists in the re-opening of old wounds. Every newspaper or market square within fifty miles of my home assaults the eye with posted advertisements for tortured flesh, advertisements that my own is meant to echo, as a casual daytime remark can rekindle a nightmare. My book is full of flaws, to be sure, but they are as nothing compared to the flaws that I propose to expose.

"Pay close attention!" my own so-called Advertisement insists.

"Trim your lanterns well. The path ahead is uneven and unpredictable. All your senses must be on the alert." Such implicit pleas, too, are part of the breadcrumb trail.

ജ്ര

> "Then why smother these burning feelings so quickly beneath a tedious heap of geographical particulars? Our lamps may well be trimmed and lit, but it seems to me you go out of your way to extinguish them. The opening pages of your book, if memory serves, meander their way through a tour of Virginia's ragged perimeter, following the compass headings, great circles, and twisting rivers that form your border. Ancient scars and tortured flesh? Figments of a dyspeptic conscience. I very much doubt if even the most alert reader could detect their presence. You throw a string of sentences around your state and ask us to plod along beside you, taking admeasurements and hunting up minutes and seconds of latitude as we go. My grandchildren can scarcely read these first pages aloud to spare my aging eyes without falling into a stupor."

Please convey my apologies to your delightful corps of readers when they awaken from their naps. Sometimes boredom has its uses, though it has its risks as well. For the sake of your domestic harmony, I will venture a defense.

By the time that I began writing two hundred years of charters and grants, compacts and boundary concessions, had fractured our eastern seaboard into a brittle configuration of artificial divisions mostly designed to placate foreign patrons, fatten English purses, or provide remote collecting ponds where the Lords of the Old World could safely deposit the pernicious moral and spiritual diseases that were afflicting them. It was a cumbersome and ludicrous machinery that the Revolution left undisturbed. To this day, the southern border of my own state constitutes the most ludicrous boundary delusion of all, defined by the line of latitude that stretches to the shores of the Pacific, purporting to appease our mutually hostile camps.

The national brawl is approaching a crisis, and our fellow citizens propose to meet it with a geographical fiction anchored by a cedar post driven into a sandbank, which shifts its shape and its extent with every Atlantic storm that sweeps ashore. A meager wooden pin that two antagonistic survey delegations spent two days wrangling over before heading west into a morass of impenetrable swamps as formless as Milton's Chaos. The earth itself made a laughingstock of our bold cartography, our fine compasses, and the pathetic navigational spider web that we have draped over the globe.

A map is the ultimate costume, after all. "Let this parcel of soil belong to the Carolina proprietors and this to His Majesty's agents seated at Williamsburg," say both petty potentates jealously guarding their respective domains and snarling at one another. I chose "Limits" for the title of my book's first chapter, just as I called its preface an Advertisement, thinking that curious titles might lead curious readers to delve beneath surfaces, to enter the cave.

"Your shipping label games yet again."

If you like. But in the case of the *Notes*, my aims were different. I told myself that if I were indeed to throw a string of sentences around a single state, any thoughtful reader would swiftly perceive the laughable presumption of our proprietary claims.

"Few readers of your book were moved to laughter by your opening pages. Puzzlement was a more common response. Look at the mix of precision and imprecision you provide! From Watkins's Point in the eastern Chesapeake, you tell us, follow a line of latitude toward the Potomac. Well and good, but what line of latitude exactly? Where is the *point* of Watkins Point? Ascend the Potomac to the first fountain of its northern branch, you declare. A mythical destination right out of Ossian! Heedless of your bewildered reader, you promptly skewer that fountain with a meridian line and stride off to the north, compass in hand, in quest of some sacred Grail. At one point you provide only approximate directions, while a few sentences later you cite the precise tenth of a latitudinal second that separates Maryland from Pennsylvania, yet another boundary fiction that your scrupulous numbers appear to mock.

"What exactly is our comprehension of longitude, as you call it? Who is this mysterious figure Cassini whose great circle computation you appear to endorse? But I spoke too soon, for on second glance I see that you simply *suppose* that we accept Cassini's authority. Suppose, on the other hand that we don't? What of it?

"I throw out these questions merely as a way of suggesting the sort of friction that is bound to plague the inaugural motions of your ingenious emancipatory machine, friction that will soon generate considerable heat once your next chapter plunges us into a list of rivers and rapids, depths and widths, bateaux and battleships, all groping for channels and feeling their way over sandbars in search of safe anchorage. As if in passing you remark that it would be easier to acquire a clear idea of these river courses by consulting a map. *Indeed, it would!* cries my frantic secretary. But do you remind us that just such a map is folded away in your end papers? You do not. A mere perversity on your part, I take it, or a casual oversight. It grates none the less. Unemancipated human nature is bound to resent your cool disregard for our needs.

"I am, however, more emancipated than most. In fact, I am quite prepared to get out my reading glass this very moment and begin poring over the schematic hints that your map provides while you carry me safely past the sucking-pot of this tedious opening catalogue."

A catalogue it is, and tedious at times, I confess, but I am delighted that the mischievous Sucking-pot on the upper Tennessee caught your fancy. As indeed it might—a whirlpool that ingests tree trunks and entire trading boats as if they were twigs and spits them up after half a mile of subsurface tumbling. Such a ceaseless gorging and disgorging of matter deserves a more dignified name, perhaps, but "Sucking-pot" captures sound and shape in a tidy package. It has no proprietary pretensions. I only regret that my map doesn't extend so far west or I would certainly have noted the whirlpool's precise location. The James and Elizabeth rivers, on the other hand, are well-established forms of cartographical flattery however indifferent most people may now be to their origins. No sea captain gives a moment's thought to the Stuarts and the Tudors while inching his way up the channel on a convenient tide. The names are pure importations and ought to have been subject to embargo.

Pagan Creek may well admit a twenty-ton vessel, as my devious catalogue claims, but its name admits little else. What notable pagan once lived and worshipped on its banks? This lost inhabitant with his unknown gods is as anonymous as the author of my Anacreontic epitaph, yet he too has left his *manes* behind. What a tangle these rivers make! So miniscule are their tributaries and so numerous their names that even a magnifying glass is scarcely able to decipher the surveyor's work. Many readers would simply settle for a bird's eye view if my written catalogue had not offered some enticement to take a closer look at the map's intricacies, arranging some of the names in the order that an imaginary bateau would encounter them as it drifted westward down the Ohio. Children instinctively take such imaginary voyages, but adults need a little encouragement to indulge their native curiosity.

As one might have expected, Indian names predominate in my long tabulation of rivers—Chickahominy, Piankatank, Hockhocking, or Monongahela—all spellings that are the work of a lettered people attempting to reproduce the speech of the many unlettered peoples who traveled these waters for centuries, speaking half a dozen different tongues. How accurate can we expect these renderings to be? Ohio is so simple a series of sounds that its three syllables seem likely to have resisted much vocal mangling, but how can we be sure? Patowmac and Tanisee—I am inordinately fond of my eccentric spelling—already exist in several variant forms, corrupting as they travel from speaker to speaker and book to book, over and over again, the way that the Sucking-pot mumbles over its wooden meals. The Tanisee even yet has two alternative names that my catalogue records—the Cherokee and the Hogohege, competing for survival. Where will the cacophony end? Can any map, however beautifully engraved it might be, hope to capture such a verbal muddle?

Even the most convoluted river has a degree of geometric regularity imposed upon it by mathematical coordinates, graphic curves, and compass points. Once its path is laid down along a grid of latitude and longitude, its appearance seems almost as predictable as Newton's fluxions. But Newton would have been the first to admit that our rivers and creeks baffle his science. Their dimensions change with every season and with the variations in rainfall that occur from year to year—now a regular flood in spring or fall and now a sudden swell that can take a traveler by surprise even in a summer drought. A century ago, the surveying party that marked our border with North Carolina had to leave the western extremity of their dividing line temporarily tied to a blaze in a tree trunk and flee to the east before autumn storms flooded the rivers and trapped them in a mountain maze where first their horses and then their riders would risk starvation. Fords can become raging rapids one week and dwindle to a trickle the next. The boundary remained tied to that tree for years before the advancing settlements caught up to it. An engraving cannot do justice to such mutability. A string of sentences can.

Is the river survey any less tedious now? I think Heraclitus would have appreciated my imperfect navigational tour past Negro Run, Marshy Fork, Ducking Hole Creek, and Piss Pot Island, places that make no appearance in the written catalogue of which you complain, though they do on the map once a reading glass retrieves them from the shadows cast by the great, ceremonial names that deface the landscape.

So many gaping mouths in those pages! The Sucking-pot is really the least of them. Small creeks like the Piankatank can barely receive a canoe, while the most formidable rivers pour out icy floods, thick with silt, through channels that can be over half a mile wide, choked with sandbars and mangled trees that threaten to disembowel any boat that attempts to explore them. How deeply do they penetrate the continent? How high are the mountains that they drain? What do a river's swiftness and the months in which it floods suggest about the dimensions of these hidden interiors? Such questions will never occur to the hawk-like reader sailing over my spacious map, but once a hawk-mind descends into the labyrinth of geographical particulars that I provide, the questions are inescapable.

The experience of descent itself is my goal—enticing the imagination to enter these countless mouths, to risk the blind voyage over unknown barriers, now fighting the current and now yielding to its impetuous force.

At some points in the catalogue, I remark how a canal here or a portage there might eventually link the great interior valleys with the Atlantic coast, but these are brief visits to the commercial surface of life, a quick glance at the endless buying and selling that preoccupy our people. Fixed obstructions abound there—not only the rocks and rapids that complicate travel, but northern winters that seal the rivers and lakes beneath ice sheets for several months each year and the possibility of northern wars preying on the flow of people and goods. The surface is a stormy zone.

The depths may impinge on infernal regions, but they can offer a measure of stillness as well, a shadowy refuge from the chaos above. When the ancients visited Hades, they expected to acquire knowledge, perhaps even wisdom, rather than to be harrowed by fear. I take them as my models. The long catalogue of rivers in my book is a cave exploration in disguise, preparation for the underworld journey that awaits in the chapters ahead.

> "I take it that we are about to turn in earnest to the engraved map that is the second of your four pictures. My secretary has already spread the sheet on a desk for our joint inspection, though much to his dismay he has yet to locate Piss Pot Island."

Then he has not descended deep enough into the map's interior. Tell him to return to my inane circle of boundary sentences for a guide and follow the Potomac toward its magical northern fountain, the one that I propose you skewer with a meridian line. Once his imaginary bateau passes Medicine Spring and Fort Cresap, advise him to look for the approach of Ragged Mountain and Great Warrior Mountain descending from the north. When he sees those ridges, he will find himself at the forks of the river, where the northern and southern branches join in their journey to the sea. If he follows the southern branch of the Potomac a handful of miles up the old Shawnee trail, he will find Piss Pot Island to be a far more beautiful destination than its name implies.

Though in declaring it to be beautiful, I confess that I am only repeating the accounts of travelers whose judgment I trust. The island's nameless namer thought that Piss Pot did it justice. Both designations are the work of subjective geographies, interior ones that call for another sort of map entirely, a resource that no reading glass can explore. The early sections of my book make this same point, though in presenting it I have probably failed to insist sufficiently on its importance.

Turn back down the Potomac now toward its junction with the Shenandoah. This singular place I consider one of Nature's most stupendous scenes, yet any European readers who sail from France or England to visit this spot on my authority might well be inclined to object to my description. "Stupendous to whom?" I hear them complain.

"The alps offer a thousand vistas of tumbled rock and raging water that vastly exceed this trivial American spectacle! The peaks and rivers of Wales, the Lake District, or the Highlands are far more impressive sights. The man has enticed me to spend my fortune and my time on an uncomfortable and perilous voyage of three or four weeks only to gaze at a natural wonder that I might easily have matched by taking a carriage ride within a few dozen miles of my own home."

A born fool makes a poor traveler. Even the most obtuse observer can plainly see that my description in the *Notes* was prompted not by an outward scene but by an inward one—a vista that the mind composes and the imagination sets in motion. The earth is an eloquent ruin, shaped by convulsive forces over inconceivable periods of time. Consider the slow accumulation of an ancient ocean behind a mountainous dam. At some point a cataclysm occurs, a volcanic eruption or an earthquake on a scale fit to annihilate Lisbon a thousand times over. The force of the water ruptures the walls of its prison, scattering the rubble aside as it carves its way to the sea. Unparalleled energy held in abeyance for millennia finds itself abruptly released, and for the next ten thousand centuries cuts a scar into the earth's tortured surface as the ocean waters pour through.

Standing at the confluence of these two admittedly modest Virginia rivers, even the most sophisticated and well-traveled observers must be prepared to close their eyes before opening them. The Missouri and the Mississippi are far larger floods, coursing through their chartless regions. The Ohio is perhaps more beautiful. But both the objective and the subjective comparisons are beside the point. The stupendous currents that I envisioned when I looked down from the broken heights of the Blue Ridge had long ago ceased to flow. The mountains had crumbled before them.

"Do I detect you once more lapsing into the idiom of the hot preacher? It can be an intoxicating role."

Not so much the hot preacher in this instance, I think, as the psalmist. You know the low regard in which I hold all English translations from the Hebrew original. The Greek and the Latin versions are far superior, but one is sometimes tempted to redress the deficiency on behalf of our own tongue. My book, I hope, is a more circumspect performance. There, I am determined to reproduce the elusive interactions between science and art, reason and imagination—the exterior and interior faculties through which we take the world's measure. They are not antagonistic avenues of the understanding. Embracing one to the exclusion of the other mutilates the spirit.

"You have mounted into yet another pulpit. Once the sermonizing instinct takes hold, it is clearly difficult to regain one's balance."

I will take a short ride through a favorite stretch of woods and clear my head.

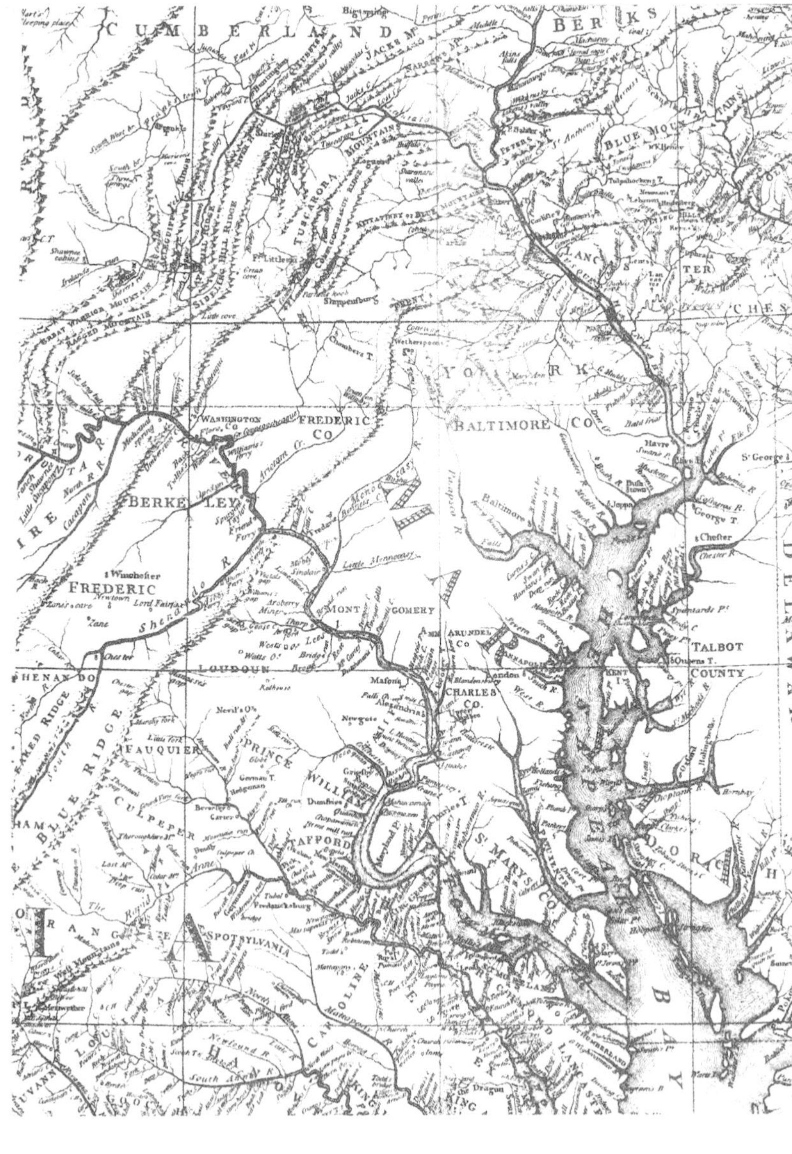

CUMBERLAND
BERKS
JACKS Mt
BLUE MOUNTAINS
TUSCARORA
MOUNTAINS
SIDELING HILL RIDGE
Shippensburg
Chambers T.
YORK
BALTIMORE CO
Baltimore
Joppa
Havre
St George
George T.
Chester
WASHINGTON Co
FREDERIC Co
BERKELEY
Winchester
FREDERIC
Newtown
MONTGOMERY
ARUNDEL Co
TALBOT
COUNTY
Queens T.
KENT I.
LOUDOUN
CHARLES Co.
Alexandria
Newgate
FAUQUIER
PRINCE WILLIAM
Dumfries
CULPEPER
BLUE RIDGE
St MARYS CO
Fredericksburg
SPOTSYLVANIA
CAROLINE
DELAWAR
BAY

Mineral, Vegetable, Animal

"While you are clearing your own head, I propose to risk throwing mine into a muddle. We have scarcely set aside your first picture and begun to take up your second, yet already I feel both bewildered and intrigued by the exhibit. Bear with me while I rouse my wits to confront the challenges of your emancipation machine. The Florentine baptistry is a music box by comparison.

"When I first retired to my farm more than two decades ago, I thought that I might actually come to miss the incessant cacophony of government. Philadelphia's bustling wharves and markets never ceased to delight me, however bitter my differences with Congress, with you, or with some truculent cabinet member angling to succeed me. Even the occasional street riot was not entirely unwelcome. You had already withdrawn to your tranquil mountaintop after the end of one especially rancorous legislative session, when an outburst of civic madness suddenly forced me to stock the Presidential sitting rooms with chests of firearms, bar my doors, and station servants at every window, expecting at any moment a mob onslaught that never came. I almost regretted the ebb tide of midnight fury and the return of public order. The few months that my wife and I spent amid the squalor of Washington City, waiting to hand you the reins of government, seemed lifeless by comparison. Not even your wrangle with Burr's minions in the House stirred my interest.

"Later that spring the flowering orchards and rocky pastures of Quincy eased my mental wounds. Not for nothing had my wife named our house Peacefield. A wren's nest she had called it when we first saw the place, decades ago, but while I had been frittering away my energies making enemies in high office, she had practically rebuilt it from scratch into a snug family refuge. My memory of the election slowly began to fade. But at the same time, I feared the stagnation that might follow such a startling fall.

"I feared dying from the top down.

"Old friends soon flooded me with books and sought out my opinions on them, as if they instinctively knew the proper medicine for my distress. I re-read all the old Wiseacres of Antiquity and laughed anew at their absurdities. Sneezing cures hick-ups, Plato solemnly assures me, the only mite of practical wisdom that dwells in the mammoth cheese of his dialogues. Like you I gave up newspapers for Thucydides and relished the change. From time to time I took up some obscure theological tome or bold philosophical treatise, and amused myself with the elaborate knots in which the authors managed to entangle themselves.

"In short, I began to fancy myself an exacting reader. Your *Notes*, however, seem destined to chasten my vanity.

"Any book could be compared to a mechanism in the sense that it is a device built expressly for the storage of ideas or feelings in all their original potency. We pick up such devices at our peril, perhaps, since the gears and springs may immediately commence work re-shaping our sentiments in unexpected ways. But the process, however subtle, is generally overt. The stakes are clear, and one may toss the volume aside in impatience or disgust whenever the urge to do so strikes. The older I get the more I find myself becoming just such a restless creature, a half-reader, and as often as not less than half, if I find myself bored or vexed by a tedious argument, a meandering story, or a fatuous style.

"On rare occasions, burning rage may sustain me through three or four fat volumes of an author's work, poorly executed though they may be, if I am on the hunt for ammunition or in the mood to collect further instances of the universal insanity of our species. I do my best not to succumb to such ignoble motives.

"But the intricate verbal fabric that you are describing to me is unlike any reading experience that I have ever encountered. The title is almost certainly facetious when one considers the scope of your aims. The complete emancipation of human nature! The harrowing of our deepest flaws! To those ends you aspire to incite a full-scale delirium in your reader. Rivers become caves or whole landscapes become a species of geomancy on a gigantic scale, vast messages written in rock and water countless ages before any eyes could possibly have been present to decipher them.

"I am prepared to credit some of the hopes you entertain on behalf of your enchanted obelisk, but the claims you make for your *Notes* go far beyond those. An epitaph, as you say, is a shipping label and needn't detain even an interested pilgrim for very long, whereas your catalogue of rivers rambles on for page after page, taxing the patience of even your most fervent admirers.

"Painters have made fortunes by rendering sublime mountain scenes of the kind you weave into your pages, but fine landscapes are an acquired taste. Even you concede, with some dismay, that many people living in the neighborhood of the natural wonders that your book describes never bother to so much as visit them, let alone stand on a rocky outcropping, close their eyes, and yield themselves up to intimations of eternity. When they encounter one of the blowing caves or uncanny gaseous vents that your book depicts, they are inclined to set the subterranean fumes ablaze purely for a lark and walk off whistling to themselves."

Well, one of our militia officers did so once, I believe. I mentioned the incident in one of my chapters but I don't think it was a popular past-time.

"Back so soon from your ride?"

The weather took a soggy turn, and I do very much enjoy your rants.

"Then I shall rant away with the greatest pleasure.

"When a book's demands are simple, or when the appetites that it attempts to address are easily stirred and glutted, then its audience is bound to be large, its reception enthusiastic, and its effects as ephemeral as a meal. The chef need not be especially skillful. Your *Notes*, however, aspire to turn an idle reader into an obsessive one, to entice us to a very different kind of mental feast, with richer dishes and rarer vintages than your friend the French envoy could have anticipated in his wildest dreams.

"My secretary, by the by, was greatly relieved to have located Piss Pot Island."

I commiserate, of course.

"For my part, I commiserate with the sophisticated foreigner who is unmoved by your sublime Potomac vista.

"You might have more success with your argument if you were to invite such a skeptical visitor on a four- or five-day journey to examine the Natural Bridge. Along the way the two of you could get to know one another more intimately, sampling the fruits of your lovely western valley, enjoying the hospitality of its prosperous landowners and tavern keepers, admiring the iron furnaces where Mr. Zane is fabricating his indestructible pots and salt pans, pausing to take in the sunset behind North Mountain. Perhaps you could offer the additional enticement of a visit to the marble quarry along the James to which your book alludes. Any traveler of taste would be eager to admire its creamy blocks and vividly tinted veins."

It is a thirty-mile side trip each way.

"So I noticed. You have probably gathered by now that my secretary and I have been soaring in spirit over your elegant map like a pair of inquisitive turkey buzzards, though of the two of us I am by far the more bald and buzzard-like, whereas he resembles a nuthatch. Only one of us really requires a reading glass.

"Our joint attention is fixed for the moment on the Natural Bridge. A head-ache-inducing abyss, you call it, though I consider the word to be something of a trap. 'My dear fellow [your European companion will promptly object] it is hardly an abyss. Your flair for exaggeration once again betrays you. By your own admission the top of the limestone span is less than three hundred feet above the floor of its little valley, or perhaps just over two hundred feet, depending on whose account we accept. Your surveyors seem to have produced two wildly divergent estimates of its height, as if the spectacle made them too a bit woozy. Even the taller of the two estimates scarcely equals the height of a cathedral tower. Impressive, perhaps, but hardly worth a swoon.'

"Invite your hard-to-please visitor to hobble his horse and scramble up beside you to the top of the arch. The two of you can saunter a moment through the pines and take in a pleasant vista of the Blue Ridge before cautiously approaching the edge of the span to gaze toward the little creek below. At that point even the hardiest connoisseur of cathedrals or veteran of alpine vistas is bound to grow thoughtful as the limestone slopes downward and the mind involuntarily begins to reflect on the delicacy of the structure underfoot.

"To be sure, the gorge is not so deep as many a well nor the streambed below very much wider than a barn door, but the view from above is certain to turn any reasonable tourist into a grave man. The distant babble of the creek and the sound of the wind passing through the trees and beneath your feet will give the experience its piquancy. Like the dramatic Potomac avulsion to the north which so disappointed your worldly excursionist, the Natural Bridge has been created over countless millennia by water and wind. The same two agents are busy even now smoothing the rough faces of the cliffs, paring away the rock that anchors the arch, attenuating the gradual curve of the arch itself. That thought alone is more than adequate to produce a headache in any susceptible viewer, listening to the whisper of invisible currents that can, over the ages, perform such titanic labors.

"Like more than a few cathedrals I can think of, the bridge is not finished. It may taper to an even more dramatic curve before fine filaments of ice and the forest's slowly insinuating roots combine to shatter the integrity of the span and reduce its lovely structure to a ruin that is just so much rocky debris cluttering the creek. An irrecoverable past and a mutable present infuse the surrounding space. Your ears take in the disorienting mixture, drive you to your knees, and prepare your reader for the burst of rapture that your book records when you regain the valley floor and look upward. The entire passage amounts to another of your cave visions, indescribable because it cannot be painted."

I thought the passage might please you.

"To a point it does. These intense inward landscapes make perfect sense to me. Even in my pitifully circumscribed old age, I have not forgotten the exaltation that mountain scenes evoke.

"But your *Notes* shift so quickly from one mental register to another, bridging the chasm between abstract analysis and emotional fervor as boldly as your limestone arch spans Cedar Creek. One minute your sentences seem appalled at the signs of a great natural avulsion capable of cleaving a mountain, and the next minute you are discussing the problem of fixing the semi-ellipsis of a parabola in a geometry exercise. From a visionary cataclysm of water and rock, lost in the genuine abyss of time, you coolly turn aside and begin comparing axis, semi-axis, and chord like a schoolboy taking an examination.

"Paralyzed by rapture you may well be as you gaze at the bridge, but in a split second you propose building a grist mill on the very spot where you stand.

"I am thinking of your book, of course, not your map or these letters. But even those documents are full of intriguing instances of verbal disjuncture—avulsions of a sort—like the farcical contrast between Great Warrior Mountain and Piss Pot Island that so amused my secretary.

"You tantalize your reader with watery siphons, whirlpools, and fiery orifices erupting from the earth—uncanny spectacles that hint at uncanny mysteries deep within the planet. Yet you are ready to brush them all aside at a moment's notice to set out on a hunt for woolly mammoths. Seams of coal buried beneath green Pennsylvanian fields have been known to catch fire and burn for decades. Your *Notes* blithely report that startling fact as if it were a mere triviality rather than a dark prophecy. "Pay that hellish vision no mind!" you cry. "The mammoths are on the move! Come along quickly. They might escape!"

"To impressionable readers like my secretary and myself, the entire earth, as your book presents it, resembles a great mammoth sleeping beneath our feet, nourishing terrible internal fires. We are paralyzed by an ominous spectacle that you seem scarcely to notice.

"Such an erratic performance is hardly a matter of complaint. An author's interests are bound to differ from our own. We are responding to different faculties of mind, perhaps, or we are pursuing different pathways of the understanding.

"But it is frustrating, to say the least, when your reader observes you wander off to watch a large hog being slaughtered or hunt up a ground squirrel to weigh while we are trying to grasp your coat sleeve to ask what cloud-berries might taste like, or wishing that you would drop your bland narrative mask long enough to reflect on the fable that the Delaware chieftain tells you of a violent clash between divine lightning and a voracious monster that was terrorizing his ancestors. And yet no sooner does the horrible creature leap the Great Lakes and disappear, than you immediately drop the anecdote altogether and begin grubbing about for tusks and grinders with which to belabor the foggy heads of foreign naturalists.

'Ah, yes," [your more obtuse neighbors might well remark], "he is certainly your man for comparing bears and otters, hamsters and moles, live cows and dead hogs from continent to continent. You will enjoy his speculations about shell deposits high on mountain peaks and the long lists of esculent, ornamental, or medicinal plants that he means for you to admire. One would think he had just this moment stepped off Noah's Ark and was bent on delivering a full inventory of the cargo.' Such dismissive jokes were popular among our urban wits not long after your *Notes* appeared. They are hardly worth serious attention.

"Many well-disposed readers, however, are still likely to be puzzled by your manner. Unlike my secretary and myself, they will not have the guidance of your correspondence to assist them on the arduous journey toward complete emancipation. They may miss a breadcrumb or two and lose heart. Have you made any provision for them?

"I have a notion that I could provide an answer to my own question, but I am more interested in your answer than in my own. I await your clear-headed response."

ﻉ

My response would have begun with the Natural Bridge if you had not already given such an able account of its impact. You and your secretary are formidable aeronauts. I am not at all sure, however, that I accept your unspoken implication that the owner of a grist mill is incapable of feeling rapture at the sight of a limestone arch soaring above his water wheel. While the millstone grinds away and the miller studies its progress, his mind is bound to wander. His eyes will occasionally drift toward the sparkling surface of the rushing creek and its singular gorge. True enough, the only abyss to be seen is the deep chasm of the ages that are required for a ridge of solid rock to take such arresting form, but I see no reason why a miller should not feel the chasm's presence every bit as deeply as you or I. Many people can indeed display a remarkable indifference to the world's stupendous spectacles, but perhaps all they require is some friendly traveler to entice them to the brink of wonder and permit them to take a look. Who named the cloud-berries after all? Not a wandering philosopher. To those learned souls the little plant with its ethereal fruit is *rubus chamaemorus*, euphonious enough as botanical designations go, but not a name likely to awaken any deeper appetites.

You profess to be surprised at my enthusiasm for hunting mammoths, as if I genuinely expected to find such a creature thundering through some rocky mountain meadow far to the west.

Why not, for once, indulge the imagination? Like any mental faculty, it has its uses. Even the Delaware chieftain could tell you that the great mammoth bull in his story was doomed. True, the beast shook off the Great Spirit's lightning bolts as they struck his skull and escaped over the northern lakes, but he must sooner or later succumb to age and isolation. No mate survived to flee with him into the wilderness. In the ordinary course of events, his species must have come to an end. He exists not in nature, but in memory and in myth. When the tribal delegation paid me a visit decades ago, both of our peoples were under assault from monsters in the form of mercenary war parties prowling the forests, mutilating and burning white and Indian alike, all in the pay of northern invaders. The purpose of our conference was to make common cause against these depredations.

But at the end of our deliberations, I took the opportunity to inquire about the gigantic bones that hunters sometimes found scattered around salt licks deep in the western forests. My guest, in turn, seized the chance to remind me that his people had been the victims of more than one ruthless invasion over the course of the ages by enemies of every nationality and stripe.

Only the most daunting totemic animal was adequate to the scope of the story. He rose from his seat to address us, adjusted his posture to the gravity of his words, and with the utmost tact implied that my fellow citizens and myself were every bit as voracious as a band of carnivorous mammoths. He said that the Great Spirit was likely to take offense at us, too, if after the war had run its course we did not mend our ways. The terrific creature was living to this day, he concluded, biding its time during the present hostilities, as avarice and greed are prone to do. What more needed to be said? I describe the scene in my book and then turn to my grinders and tusks. Such lessons scarcely require morals.

"Our flaws, then, and not mammoth trophies are on your mind."

Precisely.

When I was a boy, Cherokee delegations often stopped with my father on their journeys to and from Williamsburg to negotiate with the officers of our government. Their visits persisted long after my father's death, out of deference to his memory, respect for my mother, and mere convenience. In the first years of my law practice, as I found myself struggling more or less in vain to master the arts of public speaking, I lingered on the outskirts of one of their gatherings to hear a farewell oration from one of their famous chiefs. He was preparing to embark on a voyage to England to consult with the various ministers whose policies shaped the fortunes of his people. The occasion must have been momentous indeed, for he seemed to me to realize that he was setting out to plead his nation's cause with a parliament of mammoths.

The ring of listeners kept absolute silence as he turned his face toward the full moon, and though I could understand nothing of what he said, it was impossible to mistake the depths of feeling from which his voice emerged. Each individual mind is, in some measure, a fathomless cave.

You mention the risks my book appears to run by dwelling on mysterious shell deposits lodged atop mountain peaks or exploring the various theories that natural philosophers have invoked in order to account for a jumble of petrified tusks and teeth scattered in the forest. For all I know these may well be sleep-inducing passages. But I take much greater risks than these. One moment my reader is lulled into a state of barnyard complacency contemplating Rhode Island bullocks and Williamsburg hogs, only to find himself suddenly confronted with a virtual sermon on the customs of our native tribes, a discourse on the animal known as Man.

If our bullocks and hogs deserve a spirited defense in the court of European science, surely our people do as well, both in their imported and indigenous forms. Man, white, red, and black, as I describe the creature in my *Notes*, much as if I were considering a colorful array of domestic hens. The wording is far from frivolous.

Once my sermon ends, as all sermons thankfully do, I usher the reader back into the secular world, where two or three of our most celebrated citizens represent some of the best specimens of America's Tricolor Man in action, followed almost immediately by an elaborate tabular display of our native birds, complete with weights, competing Linnaean names, and bibliographic references that refer to entire galleries of vivid plates, a vast improvement over the four meager sketches that I am sending you. No sooner does my bedazzled audience manage to adjust to this multicolored assault than I insist on presenting them with what I term, rather coolly, an anomaly of nature: a few cases of albinism among a handful of slave families in two or three of Virginia's western counties.

What on earth can possibly justify such desperate leaps across such an extravagant spectrum of images? The breadcrumbs, as you have more than once gently implied, are rather widely spaced.

> "I assure you I was not at all concerned with being gentle. The two of us have passed well beyond the idiocies of punctilio."

Agreed. To my defense then.

Aren't all thinking people at least mildly intrigued by the subject of mammoths? The indisputable fact that such beasts once roamed our wilderness seizes the attention of even the most cold-blooded spirit. And not mammoths only, but meat-eating ones, if we are to believe my Delaware informant—nimble predators rather than the lumbering herbivores of the African plains. Why not assume for the sake of argument that even now these extraordinary beasts may lie hidden in some northern forest?

Fossilized shells have been found on Andean peaks, three miles above the level of the sea! What inconceivable conjunction of planetary energies could have elevated an ancient ocean to such heights? The Noahic flood itself could not have done so, even if the entire atmosphere had suddenly liquified and fallen to earth. Yet there the shells are, locked in their stony beds. European savants have struggled to explain the phenomenon. None of their hypotheses withstand scrutiny. A few, in fact, are laughable. Who can resist brushing these impertinent speculations aside and the speculators along with them?

As my pages bluntly insist, wonders abound in the natural world. Our ignorance of the planet we inhabit yields only by increments to the exercise of scientific drudgery. This unwelcome truth may help explain the dogged persistence my book displays in cataloguing rivers, sorting lists of vegetables, tabulating the weights and names of countless animals and plants in pathetically tidy columns—all the irrational pleasure that I appear to derive from taking the ark's inventory as you put it.

For every tantalizing cloud-berry or flickering blue bird in my pages there is an overabundance of Latin gibberish sufficient to vex even the most generous-minded reader, perhaps even to the point of abandoning the book altogether. But just when the risk of abandonment seems most acute, I introduce some unexpected avulsion. A burning bed of coal or a sublime natural bridge might do the trick. At other points I might gaze into the depths of some mysterious pools buried beneath a limestone ridge, set out on a mammoth hunt, or thrust a long passage in French from a famous Paris naturalist beneath the nose of my semi-educated neighbors, hinting at its inflammatory contents.

My pages make more than one nimble leap from brute animals to human ones without so much as the courtesy of a transition. I need to break through the complacency that dulls the perception of my readers, to limber up their joints and prepare their minds for the unusual exertion.

"Granted. But since the need is so urgent, why not translate the inflammatory French you mention? Why not make the source of your sudden determination to deliver a sermon abundantly clear by exposing the arrogance of the assault? Citing two lines of Greek in your bedside memorandum is a pardonable eccentricity, perhaps, but quoting two long pages of French prose in the middle of your *Notes* while cavalierly ignoring the needs of your English-reading audience is likely to produce some grumbling at the very least."

What is wrong with a little productive grumbling? Or worse than grumbling for that matter? Many of my readers will have already taken up my book exclusively in search of political ammunition. "Aha!" they are likely to exclaim with immense satisfaction when they reach this long stretch of French, "the whoremaster of Paris reveals himself!" Why not stir up these latent powers of resentment and charge them with energy, even if the initial gloating proves to be at my own expense? What my *Notes* need most of all are impassioned readers, not lethargic ones. As you point out, I have filled these opening chapters with a long litany of wearisome geographical and zoological detail that invites, at the very least, a modest dose of ridicule. Now it is time to break the spell.

"What is all this flummery about *le sauvage du nouveau monde* and his *petit* organs of generation?" my impatient reader exclaims. "Small wonder our minister cautioned me against this book. Petty organs indeed! No reputable writer quotes so much French. Ah! Here we have it in a nutshell. *La physique de l'amour.* One hardly needs a translator for that little tidbit. Then the passage goes on to discuss women and infants without pity or *reconnaissance*, whatever that may mean. *Les puissances de l'amour.* Yet another of the lascivious phrases we have come to expect from these Jacobin atheists! Valiant lovers? Amorous jousting? Who knows? Once we scramble back to firm English ground, the man tells me that what we have just read amounts to an afflicting picture. I dare say he's right. Let's see how he goes about healing the affliction and restoring the honor of human nature. I'll have to dig up an acquaintance who reads French to fill in the details later—a trustworthy clerk or a schoolmaster, perhaps—but meanwhile I will press on to consider this survey of man, white, red, and black, as the author puts it. That is at least one more color than I was bargaining on. Where can these pages be heading?"

These pages, in fact, take direct aim at my querulous neighbor, a different audience entirely from the one the French envoy envisioned when he drew up the questions my book addresses.

Particularly once the war came to an end, I determined that my own countrymen must be my readers—not my closest friends only, or even educated people in the main, certainly not fluent Francophiles or competent Latinists. Literate citizens of every type and every party might be expected to delve into my *Notes*, if only for the sake of catching their author indulging in some exotic vice that they might turn to political account. I began to design my emancipation machine accordingly, employing practical baits here and there of a sort that a skilled farmer might savor but not forgetting to consider the interests of merchants, land speculators, lawyers, idle tourists, invalids, architects, philosophers, or historians.

My monthly tables of temperature, rainfall, and prevailing winds are, I admit, fussy to excess, especially when considering that I assembled my data in the depths of a desperate Revolution. But who does not take a passing interest in the weather? When bitter enemies can agree on nothing else, they can find common ground in a refreshing breeze or commiserate over a killing frost. We had a pressing need for common ground, after all, long after foreign invaders had largely departed and the comforting illusions of normal life began to work their softening ways. The confederacy congress could barely summon a quorum to ratify the treaty of peace that you and your two colleagues had exacted from England. Paying our legislative expenses was out of the question. We were in danger of becoming a global laughingstock. A diet of sober fact seemed necessary.

To adapt your cookery metaphor, then, I mixed the dishes that my book was preparing to serve and slipped in recipes of my own to surprise one or another of my guests. The bit of French you complain about is on the order of an appetizer. The paragraphs of plain English that follow are the main course, as substantial and nourishing a meal as I can contrive to fit into such a small space.

Initially, I appear bent on correcting a set of cruel fables about the character of our native tribes, fictions so egregious that I would not bother to render them in English. So far so good. But within a sentence or two the scope of the discussion almost insensibly expands to all of human nature, crossing all racial divides, a chasm that I propose to bridge as surely as my limestone arch bridges its gorge, or as the continents themselves must have once been fused in that frozen northern wasteland where the mammoth sought a final refuge.

The Man of America who happens to be predominately of the red variety differs from his fellows in matters of circumstance only. Our collective natures, I insist, are the same. A culture of hunters marked by a peculiar division of labor may well result in what appears to us to be the degradation of women. It may produce different concepts of honor, of bravery, even of justice, but not different human beings. Diet influences fertility but it does not alter the delight that parents take in their children or the grief that they feel at the loss of a child. The absence of letters does not mean that poetic gifts and potent oratory are wanting in a community that must preserve them by memory alone.

The Man of America is universally prone to fear, to rage, to vanity, to pride, to courage, to piety, and to sorrow, regardless of which outward form he may take. I have known parties of Indians to appear in my neighborhood, seek out with unerring accuracy the graves of their ancestors, and mourn over their remains long after the forest has reclaimed their lost villages and full-grown trees have over-run their burial mounds. My *Notes* bear witness to these expressions of timeless grief. Our traders intermarry with Indian women and raise large, healthy families. The tribes on our southern and western borders have formed a political polity not so different from our own, taken up agriculture, and established settled towns. It is true, on the whole, that the tribal elders make do with very few laws and few means of formal coercion among themselves, but are we the happier for our elaborate governments and fortified prisons?

I could sometimes wish that an ocean of fire separated us from our European forebears, but despite the terrors of frontier war, I have never desired to quarantine the nations of North America behind such a drastic obstacle.

Will a pragmatic reader who is delighted by my lists of livestock weights experience an epiphany as he turns these pages? Will he suddenly feel an intimate affiliation with the Man of America in all the variety which that compound entity presents? I am not so naïve as to expect such an outcome. Our frontier populations and the Indians among whom they live are bound to a cycle of mutual atrocities like Ixion on his hellish wheel. For my part, I may have mounted a spirited horse and galloped furiously ahead down the road toward the complete emancipation of human nature, but I am only too aware that my reader is still crawling on all fours far behind. When I mention that our traders speak fondly of their Indian wives, and treat them kindly, do I suggest that the unmarried daughter of some western settler might do well to consider a Creek or a Delaware warrior for a husband? I do not. Do I deny all racial distinctions? All differences among the tricolor man of America? Only a fool would do so.

But I do draw a sharp line between superficial contrasts and essential harmonies; between the costumes we wear and the people we are, the people we mean to be. For the first time, in this portion of my book, its innermost springs and wheels begin to move. The reader whose energies and resentments I may have stirred will have no difficulty detecting the change. *Homo sapiens europaeus*, the Linnaeans crow, adding for good measure an entire mythical menagerie. *Homo sapiens americanus*, *asiaticus*, *afer*, or *ferus*. All pseudo-scientific masks for bigotry that the tri-color man of my book repudiates. Human intelligence and human feeling alone constitute what sapience we possess. In time they will bring about our full emancipation.

"You have yielded to the hot preacher yet again."

The subject appears to me to demand a measure of heat.

Do the generative powers of Nature favor one continent over another? The proposition is ridiculous on its face and collapses utterly once I begin throwing tapirs, jaguars, bison, beaver, mammoth tusks, and baskets of ancient teeth in its direction. Like Pinckney's withered seeress, I am an adept with bones, though rather than read them I am inclined to use them as artillery. I am not, however, indifferent to their evocative power.

Many years ago, I opened the remains of an Indian burial mound in the Rivanna bottom lands near my home in order to settle a debate among my neighbors, some of whom had been busily engaged, year by year, plowing the ancient barrow into oblivion. This philosophical inquiry, too, appears in my book, though I make no attempt to reduce its conclusions to tabular form. Is this heap of earth the relic of an old battle, a monument to the unbridled ferocity of the tribe that built it? Or was it the common place of interment for a peaceful village? In the course of confirming the latter conjecture, I briefly held the translucent jawbone of a teething child in my palm and mourned the loss of my little, nameless son and infant daughters.

The dead in the barrow were jumbled together, not by haphazard like the mammoth remains near the salt licks, but carefully layered, as if they had been brought together at distinct times, added to a common bed, and separated by blankets of earth. They had no need of obelisks and epitaphs as testaments of their humanity.

In putting my case for the Man of America as forcefully as I thought wise at the time, one critical passage that I wrote infringed on my own standards of equity and truth, but that is a subject that I reserve for consideration when we turn to the matter of Logan's eloquence, to the massacre at Baker's Bottom, and the fourth and final picture in my exhibit.

At this point in our consideration of my verbal machine, the oratorical gifts of a Mingo warrior are not at issue. We have only just unfolded the second image and given it, at best, a piecemeal look. Meanwhile my innocent readers are lumbering ever closer toward the edge of an abyss more daunting by far than the lip of the Natural Bridge, one for which they will have no preparation. Indeed, I have sought to blind them with several pages of meticulous information on nearly one hundred species of birds, listing their Linnaean and their English names along with page references to the published volumes of celebrated naturalists, gifted painters every one, so that curious bird lovers may pass judgment on the accuracy of their colors.

In the past you have accused me of smothering the powerful feelings that my book sometimes elicits beneath cascades of tedious particulars. Here, I confess, I appear to be doing precisely that.

"Except in this instance the particulars are far from tedious. To be sure many readers will give your delightful aviary only a brief glance before stifling a yawn and skipping ahead to the next paragraph or the next chapter that promises to hold some interest. Your neighbors are, above all, a practical group.

'The man had my attention for a while during his discussion of Indian life, and I was delighted with his praise for Rittenhouse and Washington, but I have never understood this aesthetic preoccupation with birds beyond a reasonable interest in roast turkey or pigeon pie. And I am certainly not inclined to delve into a sheet of tables on turtle doves and titmice when more profitable topics must lie ahead. The book seems positively determined to dawdle along as if we hadn't a care in the world.'

"I don't share these reservations, of course, but I do have an intuitive appreciation for unemancipated mental processes.

"Clearly you intend these bits of scientific bookkeeping to illustrate the necessary drudgery of careful observation as opposed to the intoxicating delusions of unfounded theory, the temptations to which your French naturalist succumbs. It is a point worth making.

"But this elaborate table of birds is hardly a hoard of innocuous facts. Indeed, it is scarcely a table at all. The flighty creatures themselves appear to have broken free of your columns and rows, rushing out in all directions, much as they do when they burst from hiding as I walk through my fields and orchards, leaving an occasional feather fluttering behind. You list their common names in no discernible order—not by size or habitat or region. You do not alphabetize them or group them by Linnaean designation. Four of your columns are the careful work of a natural philosopher, cross-referencing sources and species. The fifth is a living delirium, a flock of all the flying creatures your ordinary countrymen might recognize in their ordinary country language, soaring and tumbling across the sky.

"You may well have meant to soothe the powerful feelings that your previous pages evoked by bathing the feverish reader in a flood of cool detail, but in this instance the details seem to have other intentions, as birds often do."

For a man with failing eyesight, your vision is remarkably keen! If I had laid out these remarkable creatures in an ordinary specimen cabinet, you might never have responded to the table in such a penetrating fashion. It would never have occurred to you to distinguish the tedious columns from the delirious ones, to recognize the clash between scientific detachment and artistic ecstasy. You would never have detected the constraints of a cage or an aviary in the grid of lines that compose the table itself. You might never have re-lived the explosive flight of a pheasant as it breaks from concealment, startling the hunter and baffling his aim. The birds would have been properly labeled and grouped, but they would have all been dead.

Even so there may be more order to my chaotic column of popular names than at first meets the eye; not a scientific arrangement perhaps, but an emotional or a psychological one.

The list starts with the Field martin not because of its size—though as a class it contains countless types—but because the most common of its common names is the Tyrant Bird, a suitable beginning for a group of one hundred species that ranges from the largest winged predators down to the timid Whip-poor-will, lamenting his enslavement.

In between these extremes, the list is a dazzling palette of color—blue jay and purple jackdaw, white bill and red crest, gold wings and yellow bellies, brown curlews and snow birds, the fox-colored thrush and the painted finch. There are black caps, yellow rumps, gold throats, and red eyes glancing past as the reader scans the column, trying to adapt to the visual blaze, coping at the same time with the sudden imaginative flights that occur within the space of a single line separating kingfisher from pine creeper, humming bird from wild goose, ground dove, and sky lark. The aviary is indeed a feverish spectacle, but so rich a one that few readers who take the trouble to explore it would willingly recover their senses and return to a more impoverished world.

Yet that is precisely where I take them, in the most dispassionate language that I can muster. Over the span of a single sentence, a most unnatural bridge, I blot out the Greatest grey eagle, the Yellow-legged snipe, the Whistling plover, and the Red bird, replacing them with the pallid, cadaverous white of seven albino slaves, six women and one man, four of whom I have known myself and three by report. I group these few ghostly beings with my catalogue of indigenous animals, just as I have the Man of America, white, red, and black. But in truth they require a category all their own.

A handful of circumstantial similarities unite them, their skin, their hair, and their tremulous eyes, exquisitely sensitive to light. Otherwise, their faculties are perfect, their minds shrewd and quick, their powers of apprehension strong.

Five of the women have married and born children, one albino child and the others black, all fathered by black men. Two of the women are dead. The man is advanced in years, tall of stature and, so far as I know, wifeless and childless. Some belong to Colonel Skipwith of Cumberland County, some to my Albemarle neighbor, Colonel Carter. One is owned by a Mr. Butler and lives near Petersburg. Another by a Mr. Lee of Cumberland. These details too are a form of bookkeeping. In passing I mention a Negro man who in boyhood developed a white spot on his chin that overspread his face as he grew older. It has not affected his health or strength. I know of him directly, not by report only, but I do not name his owner.

None of these eight people have shown any sign of disease, excepting only their weakened eyesight, which even so was only a daylight handicap. In darkness, they see more clearly than we do.

"I remember the passage. You turned from these seven singular portraits to a discussion of honey bees and some idle speculation about a frozen land bridge somewhere in the northern latitudes that must once have united the continents. I may have put the book down just at this point, or given it to my wife on whose heart and head, as you know, I relied as long as she lived. My own mind was at a standstill."

And what did she say? Or did she too put the book aside?

"She said the women who married must have taken comfort in partners whose eyes could accommodate the light. She pitied the lonely old man."

Then she looked past the landed gentry with their titles and their property claims as if they were invisible and entered into a shadow life. Only a very few readers have found themselves able to follow her lead, to trim their lanterns and adjust their eyes to the darkness. But I do not regret the risks that the passage takes. As with the bridge of rock and ice that united the frozen continents, only creatures equipped to survive the transition zone were able to make the crossing. Others, even old friends like yourself, were paralyzed by the cold.

Populations, Constitutions

> "It must have occurred to you that your words might strike many readers as a confession of gross inhumanity. For a fleeting instant you imply that people and insects are equivalent objects of scrutiny. The wonder is not that I put the book down but that I ever picked it up again. Honey bees, for heaven's sake, the white man's fly! Did you suppose that a few sentences about these invaluable creatures would sweeten the bitter passage that you had just written, like Samson's conundrum about a hive in the head of a lion? If so, then you did indeed blind yourself with what you take to be the dazzling promise of natural science."

I DID NOT CONSIDER SAMSON AT THE TIME THAT I WROTE, at least not consciously, but the allusion is not without interest. Samson, too, dealt in riddles that his listeners often failed to grasp. When he slew his thousand Philistines, he struck them down with the jawbone of an ass, as if foolish words, proud theories, or verbal arrogance like that of my French naturalist were, in effect, deadly weapons that could be turned upon those who wielded them. In time Samson's enemies gouged out his eyes, but he was able to span the gap between two stone pillars, like the cliffs on either side of Cedar Creek, stroke their rough surfaces with his hands, and bring down a rain of stone upon the heads of his captors. I quite like the comparison, straight from a Boston meeting house.

> "Your man with the white birthmark, then, is a Nazirite whose strength grows as his mysterious skin anomaly does, overspreading his face like Samson's hair. Is that how your method works? By the same reckoning the tremulous eyes of the albino women signal not a weakened sense but an enhanced one, having the gift of penetrating darkness in all of its forms. Would such a gift equip them to

penetrate the hidden chambers of this passage, to unearth the veins of sympathy that you have buried there? I have grave doubts.

"My wife may have been able to intuit such meanings in part because of her warm feelings for you and for your motherless daughters, but I cannot credit them. The avulsion in this instance is too drastic. Your discussion of the brilliant aviary that you had assembled took me back to your book's table of birds with renewed pleasure, as I scanned the column of popular names with my reading glass. But your account of the six afflicted women struck me like a wintry blast. As you so deftly suggest, I could not cross the frozen bridge.

"The delightful affinity you propose between the delusions of a loquacious French naturalist and the jawbone of a voluble ass poses no such difficulty. I hooted aloud when my secretary read me that remark and alarmed the entire house. They thought I had succumbed to an apoplexy.

"When I was a boy, I loved repeating Samson's riddle over and over to myself, striding about the kitchen on a rainy day and interrupting my mother at her chores, as I declared in my most solemn tones, 'Out of the eater came something to eat. Out of the strong came something sweet.' Or is it the other way around? I probably ran the verses together over and over so often that I scarcely knew which end was up, treading out the meter and uttering the magical words until my mother must have feared that I had lost my wits.

"It occurs to me just now that you, too, like Samson, have tied torches to the tails of three hundred foxes and set them loose in the wheat fields, a pack of wily incendiaries whose movements and purposes defy even your own control. Such solitary and elusive creatures, as well as such clever ones! Reddish fur and perpetually alert, not given to a great deal of doggy noise or vulpine howls, just an occasional sharp yip in the night followed by a stealthy silence. Can the fox, perhaps, be your totemic animal? Before your hair lost its natural color to the frosts of time, the comparison would not have seemed far-fetched. Some passages in your book seem expressly intended to scorch the earth, condemning us to a kind of starvation amid your lush orchards and esculent vegetables.

"How on earth could Samson have caught so many foxes, or having caught them how could he have affixed torches to their fluffy tails without burning the creatures to death? Children are perfectly content to accept virtually any tale that includes fabulous feats of strength, but their admiration is usually quite literal. The idea that Samson need only shake himself to escape his bonds never struck my boyish mind as a symbol of his mental prowess, his ability to see through the crude plots of his enemies. But what better way to depict a master of riddles than to celebrate his ability to entrap any number of foxes and make them instruments of his will? The notion that these deeds were fables and not facts never occurred to me. I was unusually gullible in my early years and have not advanced very far beyond the level of literal thinking even now, the better part of a century later.

"Why three hundred foxes precisely? Why not one hundred or five hundred? Such questions would keep me muttering to myself in bed at night until I fell asleep. Other than possessing an ingrained fondness for rhyme and rhythm, I appear to have been born with a turgid imagination. Clearly I am not the kind of reader you require."

On the contrary, you are exactly the reader I hoped for. A hooter, a mutterer, an active brain, prone to raucous assent, yawning boredom, and the quiet, thoughtful scowl of disagreement, often registering all three reactions within the space of a few pages. Even your wife, with all her reserves of forbearance, would have recoiled at the air of inhumanity in my description of the lives of the albino slaves.

But her dismay at my callous manner would not have tempered her sympathy with my subjects, her interest in the hidden nature of their lives, her concern for their families. If anything, her feelings would have been enhanced by my own apparent indifference. The passage is not unlike the Sucking-pot on the Tennessee, pulling my book into an emotional vortex, hurling it against a gauntlet of submerged rocks through dark pools and coils of turbulent foam before spitting it out into the dead water below. And the next section of the book is dead water indeed, with thousands of temperature readings, weathervane consultations, and barometrical variations, adrift in a lazy eddy. Within a page or two of introducing the albino women, I am engrossed by climate analysis and boll weevil infestations! Your wife must have found the cruel transition excruciating.

I should hasten to add that I am neither surprised nor discouraged by your own skepticism. Breaking up old structures of belief is bitter work. I mean for my pages to serve as a kind of moldboard plow, edged with steel, fit for turning up the stiffest soils and making way for a fresh crop. A number of my neighbors are very stiff soil indeed.

> "No doubt you mean to burn away the weeds and tares as well? Samson's crafty foxes once again?"

First you refuse to credit my hidden intentions, and then without the slightest warning you embrace them. If I didn't know better, I would conclude that you have set aside your literal imagination for the time being and adopted a mystical temperament.

But perhaps I can direct your generous instincts toward another calculated avulsion built into my verbal machine. I am thinking of the queer observations that unexpectedly intrude on my discussion of population growth. In the course of sifting through a century of records, I have found it easier to portray the Indian nations living in and around our borders than to describe our own higgledy-piggledy people. Our understanding of these extraordinary neighbors is more finely grained than our understanding of ourselves. Not a surprising disparity, perhaps, given the elusive and often painful nature of self-knowledge. The gods never intended the Delphic admonishment to be comforting.

The only tables in the *Notes* at all comparable in scope to my chromatic aviary are the ones that I devote to the forty tribes residing within Virginia when the first English ships arrived, and then to the nearly one hundred more whose names I collected from four detailed lists recorded, at long intervals, by trading agents and militia officers. These tallies contained useful population estimates, along with the whereabouts of each tribe's chief towns and villages.

For the three great Virginia confederacies, I decided to display what I had been able to discover in a schematic map. The Powhatan peoples living along the seacoast line the right-hand margin of the table—its "eastern" edge. The Mannahoacs and Monacans who live to our north and west are arranged partly across the top of the page and mid-way down the left-hand margin, much as they would appear if I were to superimpose the locations of their villages on an outline of the state. The columns list each confederacy's subsidiary tribes in north to south order, descending from the top to the bottom of the table, adding the numbers of warriors that our earliest settlers thought each tribe could muster, either for alliance or attack.

This knowledge is at best imperfect. I am half-ashamed of the attention I lavished on its tabular arrangement, as if I were trying in some way to conceal my incalculable ignorance with a veneer of pseudo-scientific vanity. The energy might have been better spent trying to enlarge on the cursory records we have kept of the languages the indigenous people spoke when the English first settled the seacoast, a legacy so varied as to confirm their great antiquity in the land. Many of their distinct forms of speech are utterly lost.

In consolidating this information my motives were anything but disinterested. The neighboring tribes have long been invaluable commercial partners: suppliers of pelts, purchasers of goods, and guides to their native forests. They have been, as well, formidable enemies and crucial allies. It was in our own interest to know who they were, where they might be found, how numerous they might be, and how best we might communicate with them.

But surely we had an interest in keeping equally detailed records of our own numbers as well. Tribal affiliations we might lack, particularly in such breath-taking diversity, but for a century or more our emigrants have arrived from every corner of the British Isles and from not a few places of origin on the continent. The Dutch, the Swedes, and the French at least have representatives settled within our borders. Sectarian New Englanders in search of warmer climes and friendlier soil have made their way down the inland valleys and into our mountain coves. Our leading men once contemplated bribing entire towns of thrifty Swiss to take possession of our vacant back country and set an example of agricultural industry to our feckless frontiersmen. The proposers never carried out the plan, but it had much to recommend it.

Do I touch on any of this variety in my book? I do not.

One of my more parsimonious tables refers only to "settlers imported," as if they were all so many bolts of cloth or tuns of wine. I say nothing at all of those people imported against their wills from Africa, though the idea of importation could hardly fail to bring them to mind. The curious term "tythes" in our census figures amalgamates white and black into a single taxable category including free males older than sixteen and slaves of both sexes who are above that age. I am at a loss to explain either the policy or the word, but the fact of the amalgamation alone is sufficiently arresting to give any thoughtful reader pause.

Despite a thorough ransacking of militia rosters and ship manifests, my population tables are composed of as many blank squares as there are squares filled with reliable figures. The half a million and more inhabitants I claimed for us when the book was published were largely conjectural people. I conjured them up out of ratios and improbable assumptions—that the number of males older than sixteen, for instance, invariably matched the number who were younger, or that the number of free female inhabitants exactly equaled the number of free males—a Noah's Ark fantasy!

An ordinary bookkeeper in a modest shop, going over these pages, would be forced to conclude that their author had lost his mind.

As in some degree I have, for at one moment I am recording our annual human importations for the last century and more, arriving at the conclusion that our numbers double every twenty-seven years, and the next moment in a fever of anxiety I am proposing an embargo on immigrants to prevent our having to absorb shiploads of foreigners whom I solemnly declare to be irredeemably corrupted by life in Europe's absolute monarchies. Such people, I suggest, are bound to be licentious. Once they settle down on farms, begin to vote, and are called to jury service, their manners and morals are bound to warp our laws. Their children will refuse to learn our language. The state will degenerate from a homogeneous and harmonious collective into an incoherent mass—as if it were not already a sufficiently incoherent mass of entirely home-grown antagonisms. My description exaggerates only slightly the afflicting picture that these passages in my book present, slanders every bit as extreme as those offered by my credulous French naturalist, but this time the distortions are my own.

And yet within a few sentences of this deranged performance, I plead for time to allow for the ripening of our minds in preparation for the complete emancipation of human nature. At just this juncture in the *Notes*, having displayed in the space of a dozen pages the crippling weaknesses that plague my own intelligence, I announce my sweeping ideal. "He can't be serious," an attentive reader might understandably mutter.

"Let him set about the process of emancipating his own mind before he embarks on emancipating everyone else. These mental avulsions are almost too egregious to bear repeating! Would a licentious peasant degraded by life under a tyrant be at all likely to consider emigrating across a stormy ocean in order to be licentious in the North American woods? Would such a person have the resources in money or in energy to attempt such a drastic change? Would a group of skilled craftsmen from the Swiss cantons or German principalities willingly emigrate here, as this writer seems to believe, teach us their hard-won artistry, and then shoulder an axe, march obligingly off in search of free land, and leave us to profit from their knowledge? These dreams are as delusional as the fears that precede them, and yet the author's fears sometimes dissipate as swiftly and irrationally as they arise. Will the restless population of slaves already living among us, accumulating grievances and anger year by year, grow any less rapidly if we impose a duty on further, euphemistic 'importations'? Their numbers, too, double every twenty-seven years, with an exponential increase in their suffering and in our culpability. Is it likely that this moral blight will wait patiently for our minds to ripen? Won't some terrible rupture take place? Madness and reason are so entangled with one another in these words that they tumble their author head over heels every sentence or two—a sorry spectacle."

The pages in question are unquestionably a spectacle, but I am not inclined to apologize for their excesses. They are part of the same elaborate machine that I have been trying to describe as we make our way through the four pictures I have promised to send.

For every reader who sees through the irrational fears that I voice, there are ten who will nod in agreement, endorsing my suspicions and oblivious to the similarity between my own crude generalizations about emigrants and the even more crude generalizations about Indians that my book had repudiated only moments before. They will scarcely notice the implications of our natural rate of increase. The chasm between the races is invisible to them, hidden behind the arcane label of tythes, a taxation device that they will consider every bit as sensible as taxing taverns, horses, cows, and carriage wheels.

And these ten, perhaps, will have full suffrage. In any election their votes may well overwhelm those of the handful of readers who are capable of exposing my inconsistencies, mocking our ludicrous revenue system, and lamenting the brutality of our economy. What prospects for ripening can we expect ten such minds to display? Their anxieties invite exploitation by unscrupulous demagogues and party hacks, as well as by foreign governments eager to circulate slanders in the press that are calculated to inflame our differences. Once inflamed, those differences will inevitably sow chaos every bit as effectively as Samson's three hundred foxes. Isn't this the possibility that you had in mind decades ago when you described to me your dread of elections? Keep them to an absolute minimum, you advised, lest they invite corruption by our own passions and meddling by our enemies. I have never forgotten the letter. In your rugged way, you confront the most vulnerable feature in our peculiar species of government, its exposure to the unpredictable winds that swirl through the public mind—now a steady breeze that keeps us on our course and now, without warning, a hurricane that sweeps all before it.

Why else would I have made such a point in the *Notes* of the many hours I spent, during the depths of the Revolution, staring at a weathervane? The image in itself is a political cartoon, though it is much more than a cartoon as well. My *manes* would have immediately grasped its significance. We are sojourners in a Heraclitan world.

Only some profound spiritual avulsion would have any hope of transforming such readers as the ten credulous beings I describe. Would hurling the seabed to the top of the Andes accomplish the task? Would a racial insurrection open more eyes than wounds? Comparing the bulk of my fellow citizens to ripening fruit is, I admit, a wistful delusion. Like Odysseus's hapless crew, they have fallen victim to a powerful charm. Equally potent measures will be necessary in order to restore them to human form, an application of some subtle magic working from the inside out, not the other way around. The healing balm must ultimately emerge from the lion's mangled head. The mind is the stiffest soil I know, but once its rank grasses have been turned under, and some barren undergrowth cleared away, the parched ground can begin to soften in the mild air and gentle rain.

If I can frame the contours of my book properly, tempering its plowshare and curving its moldboards just so, then perhaps my words can prepare the reader's brain for a more nourishing crop. Even bigoted livestock lovers deluded by racial arrogance and a love of gain might prove susceptible to the proper application of mental magic and show themselves capable of change. A long passage in French, for instance, might seem at first as opaque as a blank wall, but a handful of teasing phrases, coupled with sheer curiosity, can convert the wall into a mirror, offering even the most obtuse readers a startling moment of recognition. A looking-glass that truly looks instead of flatters, that strips away vanity instead of feeding it, enabling an entire species to repudiate the monstrous slander that history strives to impose upon us.

The vile pseudoscience of European salons is the only instrument of foreign sedition we need fear. Ignorance ought to be the only alien whom we purge from our midst. The Man of America, white, red, and black, has a common interest in doing so, substituting the spark of knowledge for self-serving myth as surely as Franklin did when he shocked the learned monks of Paris with his vital electric fluid.

Nor are these pages the only such mirror I have tried to insert into this section of my verbal machine. Consider for instance my curious reference to "settlers imported."

Aren't we all such importations? White, black, and red alike? What reader could avoid posing the question, or having posed it, how does one avoid thinking of the hidden affinities that lie behind it, just as clearly as the affinities that are implicit in our idea of tythes? This innocuous expression, too, is a looking-glass. We are, when all is said and done, a profoundly amalgamated people. Such moments of realization are mirror fragments, perhaps, like the whimsical stars that you propose installing in my octagonal privies, but they catch the eye all the more effectively for being small and for appearing so suddenly amid the muck and tumble of ordinary matters. Taxes and census figures! What topics could possibly be less inviting? Yet here is a bit of ragged light, caught out of the corner of the eye, a glint of hope that our biases might one day collapse of their own absurdity. Let's have a closer look.

When the portrait of six albino slave women suddenly shifts to a consideration of fish and insects, even their complacent owners might be inclined to give a slight shake of the head, much as one does who suddenly emerges from a troubling dream.

The most inconspicuous mirror of all is hidden in plain sight when I end my account of our growing population by looking forward to the complete emancipation of human nature.

A sentence is not unlike a river, rippling along through calm, familiar channels until sudden rapids alert the navigator to unexpected challenges ahead. The idea of emancipation, for all the controversy that it provokes, is so closely coupled with our enslaved blacks that, for an instant, my readers will expect to meet them here as well. Instead, they will meet the slaves who are themselves, a treacherous barrier in the turbid stream, a glistening rock that they must safely negotiate or carefully remove if they are to avoid disaster. My hope is that they will take a long, honest look at the reflection, though at this point of course it is little more than a shard of bright glass. The complete image, in all its bitterness, is yet to come.

"One picture at a time, if you please. At this point, we are merely bewildering ourselves with provocative comparisons: sentences as river channels, obelisks as breadcrumbs, books as ingenious machines built out of mirrors and moldboard plows, rocky avulsions, frozen bridges, and who knows what else. Into this crazy mix, I foolishly inserted Samson's three hundred foxes, darting here and there, setting whole paragraphs on fire. Meanwhile, my secretary and I are sitting before the outspread map that you have told us is the second of your four pictures, but so far at least that notion too is just one more puzzling comparison, half bright with promise and half in shadow, like your furtive *manes*.

"'*Where are the boundaries*?' we ask one another. '*Where are the roads?*' The Medicinal Spring, according to your *Notes*, is by far the most popular of Virginia's healing waters, but though the two of us can easily find it with our reading glass, it is impossible to discover how to get there. Ferry sites appear here and there on the map, sometimes identified by the names of their proprietors. Presumably roads or trails lead to them on either side of the rivers they cross, but the roads and trails are nowhere to be found. My secretary and I were able to drift along the breezes that carried us in a southwesterly course to the Natural Bridge, but we were traveling as buzzards in disguise, a luxury that most human beings don't enjoy.

"We have both committed to memory the little list of symbols you offer in your key to mark the locations of towns, forts, courthouses, and so on, though I for one needed the reading glass to make them out. But Philadelphia with its tens of thousands of inhabitants, its paved and lighted streets, its busy wharves, and its markets, makes no more prominent a show on your map than the obscure hamlet of Raccoon, situated on Raccoon Creek a few miles downriver from the city, or Moorefield near Belly Bridge Creek a few miles to the east. Finding Williamsburg and Richmond gave me fits. The great estuaries and bays along the seacoast are vivid enough and suggest what extraordinary avenues for exploration they must have offered

> when your predecessors first began their human importations, but the mountain ridges whose slopes and valleys feed your rivers stretch across the map as if they were little more than strings of beads that a child might divide with a pair of scissors.
>
> "When my secretary surveyed from above the great rupture where the Shenandoah and the Potomac meet, he was crestfallen to find that, on the surface of the map at least, it reminded him of a set of gull tracks on an empty beach, not the monument to a titanic geological war that you breathlessly describe. I was forced to agree. Your prose offers by far the richer picture of the place, as of course it would, but that very richness makes the map appear even more superfluous—an interesting supplement to your chapters, perhaps, but hardly worth the cost of the engraving. Both of us admit to being somewhat puzzled by the importance that you attach to this unwieldy object as a vital element of your book's design. If you have mysteries that are hidden here, comparable to those in your obelisk, we would be grateful if you would point them out."

In light of your scruples, I am tempted to suggest that the map's greatest deficiencies are in fact its most useful features. Keeping my explanatory key tucked into a corner where only the most diligent observer will be likely to notice it is one way of urging you and your secretary to cling to your buzzard's vantage point as long as possible. A soaring bird, driven by the keenest appetite and equipped with the sharpest vision, has little interest in the whereabouts of churches, forts, or courthouses. Boundary lines and roads are meaningless from a great height. Even the difference between a rich city and a struggling trading post or crossroads village loses its importance the higher one ascends.

The map records a chaotic assortment of obscure and celebrated place names only because without them the reader's impatience would be insupportable. I can't account for the whimsical nonsense of Belly Bridge Creek, but our eminent families are eager to see themselves stenciled across the landscape, particularly if they happen to be monarchs or courtiers, princes or dukes, with the occasional famous legislator or general thrown into the mix. Princess Anne will find herself suitably commemorated along the seacoast, hard by her ill-fated ancestor who lends his name to Cape Henry. On my map, at least, both rest comfortably atop the truculent house of Norfolk. Richmond, Lancaster, Essex, and York are equally easy to find, strutting about in lavish court dress having just stepped ashore at the mouth of the Rappahannock or the James like players making an entrance on the London stage. You need not have a fit finding them.

As you and your secretary note with some dismay, however, these noble titles are very imperfectly anchored in place. It is impossible to find their boundary moorings. They resemble great sailing vessels ready to slip their cables at a moment's notice and head for the safety of the open sea should a storm suddenly appear.

Buffalo Swamp to the north, where New York and Pennsylvania meet, is securely fixed in place, contained in a tidy circle that marks its limits and refuses to permit it to wander about the map, ruining crops and spreading fevers. The gloomy reeds of the Great Dismal keep to their hourglass outline near the southern coast. But the same can't be said for any of the regal counties or minor principalities scattered throughout the tidewater plain. As far as my map is concerned, they seem rootless. Their lordly owners have made landfall, come ashore, secured their thirty-thousand-acre grants, and begun to cast about for people to fill them and squeeze a handsome revenue from the soil, but their names are still afloat on an unpredictable tidal flood. My key provides a nearly invisible tracing to mark their semi-feudal jurisdictions, but even a very powerful reading glass can find no sign of them among the fine web of creeks and rivers that clutter the engraving. The boundaries seem to have long ago washed away. The map is a picture of instability. It is a picture of change.

I do not mean that our counties are purely fictions, though they are largely that. At any given moment in time, they do take physical form, but that form is always in flux as their centers of trade grow and compete, and their people discover that individual voices count for less in a polity of countless individuals. They long to be heard on their own behalf. Sooner or later one portion of a contiguous community finds its interests so distinct from those of its neighbors, and its numbers so great, that it petitions the state for the right to name its own magistrates, re-draw its borders, and adopt a new name. This elemental rending and pulling is inscribed on the map's largest features. The jagged coastline itself resembles the interlaced fingers of two ancient hands, gnarled with time, locked in a tug-o-war as old as the earth. The Chesapeake Bay and the great rivers that feed it tear at the land like the talons of an enormous grey eagle. Are the mountains advancing to the east in regimented lines to reclaim a lost frontier? Or are they little more than ripples in the sand left to dry by a receding tide?

A thoughtful traveler standing on the Potomac heights that the *Notes* describe will inevitably conclude that he is viewing the geological aftermath of an elemental war. A cloud-born observer sailing over my engraving will draw the same conclusion, but on a vastly expanded scale and with a crucial difference. These sinuous contours of coastline and mountain range are not the war's aftermath but the war itself. The making and the unmaking are ceaseless, like the respirations of the sleeping mammoth that you and your secretary sensed beneath your feet. Depicting a mountain ridge as if it were a string of beads or seagull tracks highlights its mutability. As the psalmist implies, the planet is only superficially still. Given sufficient time, the mountains will tremble to their foundations.

My map exposes all of these mysteries. They are written boldly across its surface in characters that are perhaps too large and too generously spaced to read at first, much like the letters that form "Virginia" and stretch eastward for hundreds of miles from the Great Kanhaway River in Kentucky toward the falls of the York. The largest characters on the engraving virtually disappear amid the intricate chaos of rivers, creeks, and place names rushing inland on the Atlantic surge. From the hot-air balloon that is carrying you and your secretary far above the map's surface, this westward surge will prove to be its most conspicuous feature, an onslaught of detail as fine as grains of sand borne inland toward a thin barrier of ridges that has allowed a handful of names to spill over to the west.

As with any rising tide and rolling surf, its heaviest sediments are the first to settle and sink, lodging closest to the shoreline. These are the weighty names of ancient lineages, clinging like clumps of mussels to the pilings and wharves where their shipments of wine and silk, fine furniture and porcelain, can safely land. Southampton and Sussex, Prince George and King William, Delaware, Baltimore, Cumberland, and Gloucester. Some indigenous names still linger along the coast, too deeply embedded for any flood to dislodge, but they have largely retreated before the fatuous pride of the invaders. A few aliens ride a particularly potent wave farther to the west than others—Bedford and Amherst to the very foot of the mountains, Loudoun or Berkeley, Hampshire or Rockingham coming to rest in some sheltered inland valley. But the long barrier ridges themselves—the Laurel, the Allegheny, and the Blue—signal a change and impose a limit on tidewater appetites for land and labels.

More indigenous names will begin to appear on the map as your reading glass drifts to the left and passes over the Shenandoah, the Monongahela, and the Yohiogeney—all striving to retain some vestige of the original sounds by which these rivers were long known. Rude interlopers like Piss Pot Island intrude on the serenity of Fairfax Manor. Log's Town, Mingo Town, Newcomer's Town, and Cayahoga populate the forests of the upper Ohio, mixed with Turkey Creek, Scalp Creek, Fox Creek, or Grape Creek, all haphazard designations flung on the map by the anonymous occupants of a passing canoe.

The contrast is by no means as pure as I make it seem, but the naming ratios do palpably change as the eye moves from east to west, diluting the aristocratic legacy of the coast to reflect the very same incoherent, distracted, democratic mass that I elsewhere profess to fear when I propose an embargo on future immigrants. Even the daunting parapet of North Mountain—called Endless by the tribes living in its shadow—is a porous border, allowing improbable human mixtures to push up its valleys and traverse its high gaps.

Along the northern and western edges of the map lurk two or three nameless and boundless regions that I label simply "A New State." The temporary designations on the engraving are a practical solution to the flux that the map depicts, but they are productively vague as well. New in what sense? A state of what sort? How deep will the metamorphosis penetrate? What new species of citizen will inhabit this borderland? What sorts of gods will they worship, and what laws will they embrace?

Other generations must grapple with such questions, while you and I observe their efforts from beyond the orbit of the Moon. Will at least a few of those efforts reflect the influence of my eccentric machine? By that point I suspect that my *manes* and I will have ceased to care.

ꙮ

"You give yourself far too much credit for philosophical detachment. Your shadowy *manes* may well be indifferent to the trials of contemporary life, but you have often assured me that you are an enthusiast for progress, that you prefer dreams of the future to brooding over regrets, and anticipate sharing with my wife and myself a long afterlife marveling at the obliquities of the coming ages. The very prospect of such a destiny reconciles me to death.

"Meanwhile, I am just beginning to grasp why you consider the map a master guide to your master mechanism, though without the help of your commentary I would almost certainly have been unable to decipher it. Its key is only obvious once you have told me what to look for. How will you manage to instruct a generation of readers who have only the pages of your *Notes* to consult? They may pick out a landmark or two, locate the tiny circles that mark Philadelphia or Fort Pitt merely for curiosity's sake, add a new city name to the mucky fens north of Alexandria where Washington now stands, or pencil in a few of the public roads. But otherwise, they will probably shrug off your archaic spellings and dismiss the lovely engraving itself as a superseded artifact, scarcely more meaningful than a jumble of mammoth bones—the pathetic remains of an extinct race of beings.

"Two or three years after the second edition of your book appeared, one of those new states on your map took the name of the river flowing along its southern border and joined the Federal union while you were still living in Washington, tending to some of the executive duties that your gravestone inscription so conspicuously neglects.

"'Look here,' one of your many critics will surely gloat, 'the man expects us to credit a parcel of notes and tables that are already out of date! How can we trust him to weigh a vole, let alone a bullock, when he cannot even get his states straight?' But you will doubtless reply that the more completely the details of your engraving are superseded, the more useful it will become as a gauge of relentless change. We are always in need of renewal, such discrepancies seem to whisper, always in search of new states that more closely approximate what we mean to be."

If the map has begun to whisper such secrets in your ear, then my enchantments are taking hold. New states must inevitably bring into being transformations that no surveyor's engraving can possibly anticipate or record. Sky, water, and wind are seldom still, a feature of the natural world that landscape artists have learned to exploit in order to hint at the transience of things. Our social and political conventions are equally transient. How could it be otherwise? Even a shadow falling across a famous portrait converts the face of its subject into a sundial. Some hidden gnomon registers time's relentless passage, the gradual descent into darkness that will become the theme of my third drawing.

I do not mean to compare my little sequence of sketches to a grand canvas or a brooding Old Master. They are at best a very modest ensemble, a quartet of sorts, meant as a harmonic whole. Take the four apart and they are innocuous enough, but interweave them and they come to life. Much depends on how thoughtfully one views them. For that very reason, I suspect that your concern for the dilemmas of future readers may be misplaced. Remember that the second of the four drawings, the map that we have been considering, is carefully nested in the endpapers of my machine rather than emblazoned at its beginning, more like an afterthought than an elaborate frontispiece designed to entice a buyer. Instead, I have buried it away like a cryptic pirate's guide to a fabulous treasure trove.

Reading is the initiation ritual that any greedy adventurers must expect to endure, a series of trials by mental avulsion before the map will yield its secrets.

For personal as well as political reasons I am rather fond of this freebooter's metaphor. Several pages in the middle of the *Notes* describe the more egregious forms of piracy that comprise our history, beginning with the legacy of that consummate privateer, Walter Raleigh, chief governor of Assamacomoc, alias Wingadocia, alias Virginia, wooer of queens and troubler of kings, whose embalmed head sleeps even now in the velvet bag to which his widow tenderly consigned it. I confess to having a boyish weakness for pirates, not so different from your own voracious obsession with Samson, but my book puts them to uses that are far from boyish.

Like the ancient Nazirite, Raleigh too was shorn of his strength. No sooner had he disappeared into the Tower than other pirates stepped in to claim the spoil, securing from their unscrupulous king one fabulous grant after another to great swaths of the western globe, four hundred miles of seacoast and all the islands of the sea itself within three hundred leagues of land, stretching as far as the Pacific Ocean, embracing all manner of commodities and conferring upon the new claimants every conceivable form of authority, reserving only the monarch's customary share of gold and silver ore, along with some modest taxes on merchandize.

According to the original terms of this second flurry of grants, all souls willing to embark for these vast colonial domains, as well as all of their descendants, would retain the natural rights of English citizens, as much so as if they had all been born in the shadow of the grim prison chamber where our poor chief governor of Wingadocia was writing his history of the world and awaiting the axe.

Before long, the pirates quarreled among themselves, as pirates often do. The king brewed up a potent elixir of law and force and compelled his cohorts to drink it, reclaiming much of the booty that he had so foolishly dispersed among his old favorites and re-granting it over again to new ones, filling the map with still more baronial names that clustered near the sheltered harbors and estuaries, gazing wistfully out to sea in the hope of a summons to return to court. They never quite shed the air of exiles—my engraving says as much. In time, other quarrels broke out and other heads fell. A parliament of pirates briefly emerged and drove the frantic Wingadocians to take up arms to defend their rights and extort a solemn treaty guaranteeing them the freedoms of free-born English people, provided that they re-affirm their fealty to the homeland and give up a certain quantity of ammunition.

Whereupon the canny parliament agreed to forgive and forget all acts of Wingadocian resistance, in word or deed, from the beginning of the world up to the Ides of March in the year 1651. Pirates, I think you will agree, take a comprehensive view of their prerogatives and their jurisdiction.

Why give all this ancient turmoil space in my meticulously crafted machine? It provides some explanation, perhaps, for the abundance of titled houses whose names fill the eastward portion of my map. It lays bare the crude competition for spoils. But that information is the stuff of history, not of dreams. All of these grants, conventions, concessions, and acts of oblivion are a sort of kindling, preparation for a confidential fireside chat that I mean to have with my reader, a friendly avulsion you might say. As I set a match to all this crumbling parchment, it casts an illuminating ray in the direction of more immediate threats gleaming in the eye of a ravenous creature crouching in the shadows of a looming forest.

"Surely we have expelled the last of these piratical invaders from our bowels," my readers might joyfully declare. "We have built a new government, revised our old laws, and turned our eyes resolutely to the west. These old menaces are beside the point. Why dwell on the remnants of a forgotten time?"

In answering this peevish objection, I take the present to task every bit as harshly as I judge the past. We have indeed repudiated our larcenous ancestry and purged our laws, but we have neglected to purge ourselves. Human nature remains a beast with teeth and talons, ready to pounce at any moment upon unsuspecting prey. Our cougars and jaguars, white bears and wolves, are formidable enough. Rattlesnakes put a stop to as many surveying expeditions as Indian hostilities. More than once the great brown bear of the Rocky Mountains threatened to devour the corps of explorers that I sent to the sources of the Missouri. No symbolic medals or written testaments of friendship can appease such creatures. They have no interest in beneficial alliances.

But the more insidious predator we face springs from our feckless blend of inadvertence and good intentions, coupled with the haste with which we framed our new governments and charged them with safe-guarding our rights, laying our own necks on the block in the process. The sole faculty of making money engrosses our attention, with the result that we have foolishly replaced an aristocratic despotism with an elective one.

This was the case at the time that I was originally building my machine and has remained so to this day, allowing a few thousand men of property in the state's eastern counties to overwhelm the voices of those venturing into the mountains and beyond, sowing dissensions without providing an equitable means to address them. Our legislature is too homogeneous and utterly unchecked, appointing judges, governors, and executive councils as it sees fit, defining its own quorums for the conduct of business, whether four members are present or forty, and reshaping its privileges to serve the needs of its affluent masters, as if a constitution were no different from an ordinary legislative act that any subsequent assembly could modify at will.

Twice during the depths of the Revolution our House of Delegates sought to appoint a dictator vested with every species of power over persons and property, of life and of death, and it very nearly succeeded in creating such a monster out of fear that a democratic body could not effectively resist an armed invader. The advocates for this step pleaded the example of the Roman Republic, which in itself should have exposed the madness of their proposal. Man is, as you have so often noted in your letters, a Bedlamite.

These deficiencies must inevitably be corrected, if not in my lifetime then surely before the new century is very much older, at which point my book, like my map, will fall out of date. "Oh, we have handled all of that," my future readers will smugly declare. "We have looked into our flaws and taken steps to correct them. The old man's anxieties no longer pertain to our present world and the new order of things. To be sure he meant well at the time, but times have changed."

I fervently hope they will.

But representative government is a complicated mechanism in its own right. Even well-intentioned minds can succumb to a temporary crisis and surrender the liberties of the people. We made a bad government once, and we may well do so again. Old diseases recur. The best physicians keep a careful record of old treatments.

Somehow the Bedlamites must be equipped to rule themselves. They must be coaxed out of their delusions long enough to frame grand principles of government for their asylum, a grand Bedlamite machine sufficiently elaborate in design to thwart any attempts to subvert it, while responding with all the subtlety of an exquisite violin to the ever-changing dreams and aspirations of the mad. This machine must reside in an act transcendent to the will of any particular elected assembly of lunatics and unalterable by them. It must accommodate amendments as its defects become apparent, but it must not be too accommodating. The written word remains a bulwark against failures of will and of memory, but it must not be so brittle a structure as to shatter under every pressure brought to bear against it, or in the face of challenges that it could not possibly have foreseen when its various parts were first linked together in an intricate balance.

The present government of Wingadocia meets none of these tests. At one point I considered comparing it to the work of a harried seamstress trying desperately to make a whole shirt out of a square inch of linen, but I struck the passage out of my book.

Franklin, much as I loved him, often impressed me as being far too willing to reduce questions of great seriousness to jokes. But I knew him mainly as an old man—not so old as I am now, I hasten to admit—riddled with gout and perhaps too jaded by experience of the world. Can it be true that he slept through much of the Federal Convention, while the articles of the Constitution were under debate? If so, then I strongly suspect him of smiling as he drifted off. His slumber was his speech.

You, your secretary, and I, however, have now reached the mid-point of my book and vigilance is in order. We are deep in the workings of the machine, surrounded by delicate wheels and springs as fine as a human hair, by the movement of tiny pendulums and fragile escapements. It is not a place for joking.

Laws

"A timely jest is as good as a lightning rod—so Franklin seemed to believe. Laughter could defuse the most explosive factional passions, or at the very least stifle an angry outburst until cooler sentiments prevailed. Despite that phlegmatic mask of his, he had a formidable temper. I saw him fall into one or two splendid rages in France at the antics of Arthur Lee. The man had a sick mind, Franklin fumed to me one evening, after Lee had stalked out of a late supper we were sharing in a jealous fury at some perceived slight."

His older brothers were hard on him. They are by nature a prickly family.

"Your entire Philadelphia delegation was prickly! Other than yourself, of course, and perhaps Peyton Randolph before the poor man dropped dead at your dinner table. My cousin once said that he always felt he should take along a set of dueling pistols when he paid a friendly call on the Virginians."

He was being facetious, I assume.

"The Adams clan are famous for their facetious streak. I once suggested to my wife that I might be able to exert more influence with Vergennes if I allowed a lovely countess or two to perch upon my knee and kiss my nose now and then at a court levee. 'It does wonders for Franklin's reputation,' I remarked. She was not amused."

I suspect those little dalliances were all for show.

"As were his public displays of boredom at the Federal convention. Gerry told me some years later that Franklin did now and then appear to nod off during one of Hamilton's harangues, but he was convinced that the episodes were feigned. Your countryman

Madison, Gerry believed, was forced to take reams of notes just to stay awake. Hamilton droned on, the flies buzzed, and Madison's pen kept scratching madly away. I find it an amusing picture.

"Franklin once regaled my cousin and me with a little parable about mankind's pretensions to reason. 'Picture the Reasonable Man busily engaged on some philosophical experiment or weighty treatise,' he began. 'A servant knocks at his door to call him to dinner. *Dinner! What folly!* the Reasonable Man exclaims at this fleshly intrusion. *What are you having?* Ham and chickens the servant replies. *And shall I interrupt my train of thought to go nibble on a hog's arse? I'll eat tomorrow!*' At that point he laughed so hard at his own yarn that tears came to his eyes."

What was the moral?

"I am not entirely sure. The puzzled looks on our faces only seemed to increase the old fellow's amusement. I thought of him more than once as I blundered my way through our state convention a few years ago. The language in our constitution needed some tinkering and my neighbors thought I could bring a measure of *gravitas* to the proceedings. Franklin might have done so. He could utter a mild jest, drift off into a nap during some dreary debate, and wake up spouting aphorisms like a sage all in the space of half an hour. Printers, he once told me, grow accustomed to running off satires and sermons in the same afternoon. Old attorneys, on the other hand, are always searching for a stick with which to beat someone's brains out.

"I ventured a speech or two in our convention sessions, but in truth I stammered like a hapless clerk reading for the bar. *Could that fat fellow at the rostrum really be our demi-god, Mr. Adams?* the younger delegates must have asked themselves. *He hardly looks the part of the rebel now, but perhaps he was a more formidable figure in his younger days.*

"The fact of the matter is I never looked the part of a rebel. Shortly before my cousin died, he confided to me that you and I were considered to be a comical pair at the Continental Congress: the plump and scrappy Boston lawyer side by side with the tall, reserved Virginian who loathed public speaking and seldom smiled, at least when others were looking. "There go the Menaechmi," the witticism went in whispers whenever the two of us happened to appear together.

"Trumble hints at the ludicrous contrast we two made in that grandiose canvas of his. Friends dragged me to view it when it was on exhibit in Boston a week or two after I had lost my wife, hoping to distract me from my grief. The painting is the size of a respectable sitting room and makes the presentation of your American declaration look like a gathering of Dutch cigar merchants. Hancock appears to be sitting on his hands, as if he has no intention of taking up the hot potato you are offering. Franklin resembles one of Macbeth's Weird Sisters, whereas I seem about to burst from my waistcoat like an over-ripe melon. The three of us all have our hair, at any rate. Your bushy red crop, I recall, looks especially lush.

"Here I am jabbering away about a hundred things that have nothing to do with the next picture that you mean to exhibit or the role that it plays at the core of your emancipation machine. Your reference to Franklin's wit followed so swiftly by your sobering incitement to vigilance set my mind and memory in a whirl."

I was trying to be helpful.

"Then perhaps you can help me one last time to make sense of your book's splendid engraving. I see clearly enough how the obelisk's inscription might well lead a quizzical tourist to the *Notes*, and to some degree even my feeble vision can appreciate how the *Notes* help me decipher the map. But however vigorously I brush up my aging faculties, I cannot make out how the map and the obelisk are parts of a harmonic whole.

"Paper and stone seem as antithetical to one another as spirit and flesh. I cannot bring the two together, any more than I could slip your granite monument into my pocket and venture off to explore the woods."

I may have exaggerated the harmonic effects of my little exhibit. It is an author's failing.

The obelisk's location does appear on the map, though you will have to imagine the actual stone on its leafy slope. It sits very nearly at the center of the state, on the apex of a pyramid formed by the intersection of the South West Mountains with the Rivanna River. At least to my fond eye it resembles a pyramid, though on the map it forms the letter "x" as well, with Shadwell, Monticello, and Charlottesville faintly inscribed at the crossing point. One might even compare the spot to a stick man or a skeleton, with Orange

County's capital "O" standing for the vacant eye of a skull perched atop two boney legs that straddle a section of the James between Elk Island and Rockfish River.

I have pondered the map for so many years that it has acquired all the force of a recurrent hallucination, a kind of shimmering mirage that distorts distances and makes the landscape appear to have a will of its own. The third great "I" in "Virginia," for instance, spanning the center of the state, appears to brood over Albemarle within an inch of my mountain home, not unlike some monstrous incarnation of myself, an all-consuming dictator as terrible as the figure our House of Delegates once tried to summon into being. At times it strikes me as an emblem of my insatiable vanity.

How fiercely I disputed the authenticity of the Mecklenburg Declaration when that mendacious document appeared in the newspapers a few years ago! How stunned I was that some obscure parochial body in the backwoods of Carolina would try to assert its priority over our Declaration of American Independence!

As I recall, you chose to view this fantastic fraud, initially at least, as a deep mystery, but we both know only too well that nothing so mesmerizes the staring animal Mankind as a riddle, a paradox, or a deep mystery. The more wildly improbable such a thing might be, the more generous its reception. The work of the intrepid Mecklenburgians, you wrote, made Tom Paine's pamphlet seem a crapulous mass. I admired the vigor of the phrase but deplored the sentiment. Within a day or two of receiving your letter, I set to work to grind the upstart claimants beneath my heel.

No histories mention them. No contemporary record contains their spurious declaration. We might hope to discover the fiery plumes of Mt. Etna in the North Carolina hills with as much expectation of success.

I was sorely tempted to set aside my life-long aversion to newspaper quarrels and write a letter challenging the defenders of this disgraceful sham. As it happens, others took up the gauntlet on my behalf, and my temper had time to cool, but the strength of my feelings startled me. That a seventy-six-year-old man who could barely walk fifty feet into his own back garden should rise up in such fury over such a paltry thing, where no issue of life or limb was involved, no question of personal integrity, no insinuation of malice, but only the bauble of reputation at stake! Almost before I knew what was happening, I had declared war on the mythical Mecklenburgians. It was I who turned out to be the impassioned volcano. Perhaps, as you have often implied, we are never really done with the earth. Not for nothing my once flaming hair and burning cheeks. They still smolder beneath the snow.

Leave my stick man to look after his own affairs and retrace your buzzard's flight over the map, following the east face of the Endless mountains northward from the Natural Bridge. As your course takes you toward the rich meadows of Rockingham County, near the junction of Christian's Creek and South River, you will pass over a delicate thread of lettering that spells out Madison's Cave. The words are so finely rendered that one wonders how the engraver managed to preserve them. They seem to have been written with spider's silk. The cave is my third picture.

"Your third here, perhaps, but it is the very first picture in the *Notes*! The only true picture in the entire machine, now that I come to think of it, since the map that we have been poring over isn't part of the book at all but a supplement tucked rather awkwardly in the endpapers. Your final appendix, to be sure, includes a squiggle of rivers, rather crudely drawn, when you are wrestling with the Baker's Bottom murders. Surely you don't consider such a last-minute sketch to be part of your harmonic quartet? The outline of the cave is the only illustration of any consequence in the body of the book. Perhaps you should place it first in your exhibit as well and forget about your obelisk.

"Better still introduce an outline of the obelisk alone immediately preceding the long tabulation of state papers that makes up your final chapter. What a dusty inventory of ancient documents rummaged up out of an Egyptian ruin! I have no patience for such archival zeal. Surely you could consign this collection of miscellaneous citations to the tomb of time. John Cabot's first glimpses of *terra incognita* are wonderful in their way, I suppose. They would make a fine Latin epigraph to the entire book. But the memorials, reports, petitions,

> instructions, agreements, and deeds that follow boggle the mind. For page after page the inventory mutters along. Your river survey is high drama by comparison.
>
> "Even on its own merits, the list is sheer pedantry. A 'not-unuseful catalogue' you call it, which is mere jibberish for conceding that it is useless. But I would be far less impatient with this bibliomania of yours if your book had not cut the public record off a few years prior to our struggle for independence, at the very point when the tedious litany of dusty parchment was starting to reach interesting times.
>
> "At least one of the documents that you reserve for your gravestone inscription surely belongs on the list: your act in defense of religious freedom. A state paper infinitely more important than Lord Culpepper's haphazard land grants or Lord Cornbury's pompous commission. Really, old friend, as your self-appointed editor I am beside myself at this last perverse avulsion. At a certain point, authorial humility is positively insulting. Do you, in fact, want to attract readers or are you going out of your way to put them off? I could pull out what remains of my hair with exasperation."

At all events spare your scalp. My conscience is already overtasked. The idea of adding the obelisk to my pages is yet more evidence of your facetious streak. That image belongs in a private portfolio that I am sending to my oldest friend, but it is not part of the emancipatory machine.

For one thing, it is both too crude and too personal to be of much help to future readers. The drawings that the book does contain should suffice to stir their minds without requiring me to rise from my grave. I am determined, as much as possible, to remain in hiding.

The names of Monticello and Shadwell, as your secretary must have noticed, are almost too minute even for a reading glass to pick out on the map. When my book discusses the revising of our laws at the outset of the Revolution, I attribute the task to three anonymous "gentlemen" laboring away at their thankless chore. I do not disclose that I was one of the laborers. The plan of emancipation that we prepared was my work alone, though when my machine describes the proposal, I do not mention my authorship—not because I dreaded the resentment of my slave-holding neighbors but because I hoped to deprive them of any personal grounds to reject the idea out of hand.

"Oh, that is Jefferson to a fault, the American Robespierre in all but name. If he had his way, he would set up a guillotine in Williamsburg or Richmond and behead every slave trader he could lay his hands on, wipe the gory blade clean, and start in on his fellow planters next. You know, of course, that the man is a rank atheist and a keeper of black concubines?"

My only hope of getting a fair hearing from such people is to appear to be one of their number, to share their fears and their prejudices, to present myself as a bigot among bigots, if not the greatest of them all, the Arch-hypocrite of our unholy republic. We will get to this section of my book in a moment. To my own mind it is the cave in another form, the cave's essence in fact, as I think you sensed from the first moment you began to read those terrible passages. They were worth diamonds, you wrote me then, as if instinct alone had told you that I retrieved them at great cost from some fetid mental cavern and brought them to the light.

But I am anticipating myself.

When I mentioned the need for vigilance in the very heart of my machine, I meant only to stress how cautious any explorer must be who hopes to probe the soul's uncharted depths. Even the most carefully tended lantern casts only the weakest of gleams into the surrounding darkness, a luminous speckled pool that trickles through the lantern's perforated tin shield. We must be forever alert to any errant breath of air that might extinguish the candle and entomb us forever. We must keep careful track of the twists and turns that the passages take as they open before us. If we are prudent, we will stop now and then to estimate distances and trace a crude map of the sinuous path we have traveled on a slip of paper. An eye-draught I call it in my book, though mind-draught might have been a more accurate label since the mind's eye is the organ that does the seeing.

Italian friends have reported to me the intriguing discovery that bats use their ears to navigate the catacombs where they sleep, using echoes as if they were light, but we stumbling explorers must stitch together a series of fragmentary images in order to reconstruct a cave's shape as a mental whole, filling in the shadows between each puddle of lantern glow as we leave the entrance behind.

The eye-draught that I made of Madison's Cave, with little thought of publishing it and even less of fitting it into a devious machine, is the third exhibit in my portfolio. Not the eye-draught in its original form but a modified version, less a guide than an admonition.

In the fall of the year following my wife's death, I agreed to serve a term in the Confederacy Congress—more to escape from painful memories than to satisfy any personal ambition. I had hoped to join the Paris peace commission in some useful capacity, but the job was done before I had a chance to set sail. You had already forwarded the treaty draft to Philadelphia and turned your attention toward wrangling loans from the Dutch. At the time I had lost all desire to play a leading part in the daylight world, but neither could I bear living much longer in the mausoleum that my home had become. With my oldest daughter as a companion, I rode north up the valley toward Princeton, where our gypsy legislature was planning to convene for a final session before shifting south to Annapolis as winter approached.

The route took us along a fork of the Shenandoah directly beneath the mouth of Madison's Cave. I expected to join Isaac Zane in another day or two, exploring a celebrated cavern near his home before finishing our journey. Without giving the matter much thought, I decided to allow my daughter a well-earned rest with an innkeeper's family while I investigated what this first cavern had to offer. We were in the heart of the limestone country. Foolishly enough, I plunged into the cave with only a single servant as a companion, each of us with a lantern and a pocketful of candles. We spent hours charting the tunnels and chambers, naming one the Curtain Room after its spectacular array of stalactites and another the Sounding Room after its haunting echo. I had no thermometer along, but I did take estimates of the slopes that we clambered up or slid down, here a climb of fifteen degrees, there a descent of twenty-five, and recorded the changing elevations as I went, noting a gain of a dozen feet at one point, a loss of seventeen at another. The path trended downward for the most part, ending at two places in leaden pools that disappeared into the darkness beyond my candle's feeble reach.

I recorded everything I observed on a rough map—every angle, every number, and every name. None of this information remains on the image as you have it before you, the version that I included in the *Notes*, not even so much as a key to explain which of the arrows I left on the map indicate a rising or a falling tunnel.

These omissions are not so perverse as they might seem, but for the moment I wish only to call them to your attention. Ariadne's thread might have provided another kind of guide, I suppose, but how much string should one stuff into one's pockets in order to manage the job? How far will we be able to penetrate before the supply runs out? How many hours do we mean to wander through the cave's chambers? Will all the back and forth tangle the line into a knot? What if the thread should snag on a jagged column of limestone and come apart? Making a map as one goes is the more sensible tactic. It is a wonder that Theseus did not think of it, but his mind was probably intent on the monster that he expected to meet at the heart of the maze. Mine is as well, but in the *Notes* I separate the drawing of the cave from the spectacle of the monster by some hundred or more pages of miscellaneous detail, lulling the minds of my readers into a deceitful complacency. Sending not a few of them into a stupor, perhaps, as I did with your grandchildren, until without warning they find themselves at the threshold of a mental underworld. I call the chapter "Laws."

Without arousing their suspicions, I take them by the hand and lead them very deliberately but very gently to the cave's vestibule, chatting all the while about our system of county justices and their various jurisdictions, reflecting on the means we have devised to thwart judicial bias or to cope with warped minds. Everyone I have ever met, from the merest farmer or clerk to the most lordly merchant, fancies himself an amateur attorney and loves reading about legal technicalities, property disputes, rights of appeal, or the power of pardon. The unpredictable behavior of recalcitrant juries is an endless source of interest. Everyone relishes discussions of high treason, capital crimes, or felonies. It all goes into the pot where I am stewing up a fantastic ragout to entertain my readers while the gentleman revisors are preparing their emancipation amendment in secret. The ingredients of the ragout appear in no particular order and in no fixed amounts.

As we work our way slowly toward the mouth of the cave, I assure my readers that we support our poor in the houses of good farmers. Vagabonds we lodge in workhouses. Strolling beggars are not to our taste. They wrinkle their noses in sympathetic agreement.

"We rely on the nursing of neighbors to take care of our sick," I add, "rather than sending them off to die of neglect in those lazarettos known as general hospitals. But we need to consider creating some central institution for difficult cases of surgery." Murmurs of enthusiastic approval break out. A foreigner may become one of us merely by moving to the state and taking an oath. Native-born citizens may alienate themselves just as easily. Tobacco, pork, and pitch must suffer an inspection before we export them. Only the purest articles pass muster. Gaming debts we declare invalid by law in the hope of discouraging gamblers. Iron works, on the other hand, are welcome. Slaves have the status of land in our laws of inheritance, but the gentleman revisors are considering treating them like furniture. Our statutes encourage the careful breeding of livestock, as well as the merciless extermination of wolves and crows. "Such a far-sighted people," my readers might begin to think. "Such stewards of the future!"

Suddenly I snap my fingers and disrupt the verbal trance. The gentleman revisors now wish to present a plan for systematically freeing our enslaved population, followed by its gradual expulsion for unknown shores. In the blink of an eye, my *Notes* exchange open sunlight for the chill of a shadowy cave.

> "The trance was, at best, a fragile illusion to begin with. Parts of your legal ragout were simply too good to be true: the tender solicitude your citizens purportedly show for the poor and the sick, your high-minded contempt for gambling, your incredible tolerance for all manner of newcomers. All partly true, perhaps, but subject to many lapses and quibbles, I dare say. A committee of gentlemen revisors willing to consider enslaved people as furniture, after all, is not an entirely trustworthy source of information. The behavior of your juries acknowledges as much whenever they seize the reins from a presiding judge whose mind they consider corrupt and settle questions of law on the basis of their own common sense. All in all, you seem to me a confounding blend of breeders and exterminators."

We are that and more. Consider the next scenes in my pitiless performance. With the announcement of the secret amendment on emancipation, my words take an unexpected and unbroken downward plunge, embarking along a stream of ink without the respite of so much as a change of paragraph for a half dozen pages or more, and only the faintest glimmers of candlelight reflecting from the dripping walls. Disquieting echoes fill the darkness. *What is the meaning of these different skins we inhabit? How deep do our pigments go? Rosy suffusions amid a creamy white. Immoveable veils of impenetrable black. Why does the one blush and the other mourn? What proportions of shame and sorrow do they disclose?*

To begin with, the revisors propose that the state become the slaves' family, taking black children from their natural parents and their white owners as they reach school age and cultivating their various geniuses at public expense until their educations in tillage, arts, or sciences are complete. As soon as they wish to start families of their own, the amendment stipulates that we ship them off with arms, tools, and pairs of domestic animals in little arks that might lodge on some convenient, and distant, Ararat where their passengers may begin the world afresh. Once enough of these hopeful argosies depart and the older slave generations begin to die off, we can send abroad for villages of sturdy Germans or thrifty Scots to fill the gap in our numbers. This plan, the revisors believe, is the only alternative to internal convulsions and wars of racial extermination. Ineradicable prejudice and bitter memory are bottomless caverns. They will always conceal monsters.

Do the monsters have nothing to say for themselves? To be sure they do. Let the paler version speak first, once they turn away from the mirror in which they are forever admiring their fair complexions. Color, they insist, is only the first of their objections to incorporating blacks among the citizens of our new state.

"Surely you have noticed striking differences between our races in perspiration, odor, and the rank growth of bodily hair? We hear that black women have been known to mate with apes. Anyone can tell you that their men feel lust more than love; that both sexes prefer a midnight debauch over sobriety and sleep in preparation for the next day's labor; that they do not feel grief, that they make no poetry, and can scarcely be said to sing. Courage they have, but it is a thoughtless reflex, like the rage of a beast, rather than the reasonable resource of civilized killers."

So says the first set of cave dwellers that my *Notes* encounter, blinking wildly in the light of our lanterns.

To which the second set offer a wordless reply: "You may purchase our bodies but not our emotions, our days but not our nights. Our faces are the frontiers of an inner kingdom to which we admit no aliens. That our memories are strong should not surprise you. That our hearts are generous should make you dread the day in which we reclaim the immense debt you owe us for the suffering we have endured. Your own poets warn you that slaves are made, not born. Beware, then, of what you have made. All the apparatus of your proud science, your optical glasses and your anatomical knives, are incapable of distinguishing our hidden faculties of mind and spirit from the crush of circumstance that you have imposed. Analysis by fire leaves us untouched. Even your secret plan of emancipation concedes the richness of our genius, our fitness for building new worlds. You dream of removing us beyond the reach of mixture, but we are already one blood with you. We have always been so."

> "It has been many years since I read the pages that you describe and my eyes are no longer equal to the challenge of revisiting them, but I remember the passages only too well. Diamonds indeed, but their brilliance and their value are completely hidden beneath a crust of mineral filth. Your description just now has split the crust along its brightest facets and disclosed the gem beneath, but unless my memory is utterly at fault, your machine leaves the crude stone almost completely intact as you turn it over and over in your fingers, half appalled and half puzzled at what you have discovered and where you have discovered it. You can only have made the acquaintance of the first of your cave-dwellers by looking into yourself.
>
> "My wife, my son, and I discussed these pages on a carriage ride to Calais and during an interminably wet winter in London. We scarcely knew what to make of them."

Your memory is as trustworthy as ever. I have indeed distilled the contents of my inky stream to a handful of sentences divided between two mysterious voices murmuring back and forth as they wander through the cave chambers. A soft, steady drip from the stalactites overhead, or the distant flutter of a bat's wing, almost completely obscures their words, but a careful listener can pick them out as they echo off the limestone walls. It will take a careful listener indeed to discern beneath the sheer incoherence of the first speaker the latent portrait of the second. I had hoped that at least a few readers of my book might utter these pages aloud as they worked their way through them. The ear often detects nuances of meaning that the eye and the mind fail to discern until some gifted actor brings the lines to life.

There were, after all, two of us in the cave, myself and my servant, one white and one black, master and slave. We talked together quietly and infrequently as we worked our way forward, reluctant to awaken the echoes but grateful for any familiar human noise as we discussed which shadowy pathway to explore. My servant held his lantern between our two faces while I scribbled away at our map, a collaboration between two minds linked together in mutual darkness. These underground hours may have sown the seed that eventually yielded its bitter crop in the pages of my machine. Or should I say yielded up a coarse diamond which I put, unthinking, in my pocket, drawn to it by some vague promise it seemed to contain.

When I called this performance pitiless, I meant in part that it would show no more mercy to me than to the most bigoted of my readers. They are the judge and jury whose minds I must try to move. No bludgeon that I know of is adequate to the task. For better and for worse I am, in truth, the Arch-hypocrite of an unholy republic. However squeamish I might seem about the cruel dissection that my words perform, I am all the while applying the anatomical knife to myself, draining abscesses and excising tumors that I have harbored in my own flesh from childhood to the moment that I write down this sentence.

But too many of my readers will scarcely detect the knife at all, let alone apply the excruciating blade to themselves.

"Of course, our field hands are only so much muscle and nerve, and the house servants not much better, if the truth were known. What did you expect them to be? They are, after all is said and done, creatures of sensation rather than reflection. When they are not working, they are usually asleep or getting into mischief. The tales that we hear of great African civilizations are apocryphal yarns. Our Indians carve lovely pipes and make moving speeches, but our blacks do little more than pluck a banjo and tell childish stories. Now and then one will produce some doggerel verse or an eccentric letter that the northern newspapers take up, but these exceptions, poor as they are, merely prove the rule. The Greeks may well have believed that slavery obliterated human worth, but most slaves the ancients kept were white. Epictetus and Terence began life as slaves before sensible owners freed them, but they too were white. With us, manumission is practical on a small scale, perhaps, for a handful of very loyal family servants, but on a large scale the idea is merely embarrassing. At least we do not routinely torture our blacks before taking their testimony in court or expose them to die of disease or old age as the Romans did. Any master among us who did so would feel the full weight of the law."

I have overheard such opinions hundreds of times at home, at school, throughout my first years reading law, while serving as a burgess, and attending congress. I can recreate them in my sleep. But in the pages of my book, I cast them back at my reader stripped of their ugly immunities, steeped in doubt and bewilderment as even the most seasoned explorer of caves often is.

It is one thing to degrade an entire people while you are sitting in a comfortable parlor speaking with a cluster of neighbors who are nodding away in unquestioned agreement while the house servants move unobtrusively about, serving tea and sweetmeats. It is quite another to repeat the same words while you are buried in darkness, surrounded by sullen walls of oozing rock that threaten at any moment to entomb you. Ignorance and complacency are conjoined twins, with scarcely a whole heart and half a brain between them. If my scalpel can cut closely and carefully enough, I can separate the two, remove the corrupted tissue, and restore a few readers to health. At least I might have some hopes of saving myself.

That is the only anatomical knife that I strove to wield. Over the years since my *Notes* appeared, few patients have consented to endure the operation.

To complete the cure, one must first enter the cave, alone if necessary, but ideally with a trusted companion. Two lanterns give at least some assurance that both will not fail at once. One flame can relight another if the first happens to be extinguished.

The pages that you and your family struggled to understand during your dreary English winter are my map of an underworld that no child of my time and place could possibly have escaped—a maze and a monster that no hero could confront on our behalf. The Arch-hypocrite of our unholy republic, however, is another matter. What if the high-priest of equality himself were to harbor terrible delusions and anguished doubts? What if the American Robespierre were to lay his own head on the block, in the silence and privacy of the monastic library he keeps sequestered on his airy mountaintop, unleash its deadly blade upon himself, and drop his hateful nightmares into some vile receptacle for disposal in unhallowed ground? The underworld journey tends downward, it is true, but not without a handful of upward pitches that offer some chance of recovery, an end to the grim apostasy that our lives have come to represent—mine more than most.

To be sure, the arrows on my eye-draught are a confusing jumble. How can readers guard against a bruising, or even a fatal, fall if the map fails to show where the path might suddenly drop away beneath their feet? How can a party of explorers marshal their energies for a future climb, a desperate scramble toward the light? Is any portion of the journey redemptive? My drawing implies a solution to this last question in the two scarcely noticeable breaks that divide the cave's continuous wall, gaps that mark where two quiet pools disappear into the darkness. The scene is Stygian, I know, but these shadowy bodies of water are not turbulent rivers over which a dreadful ferryman carries condemned souls. They are untroubled by surface disturbances, by droughts or by floods. Their water is always cool. If they are indeed linked in some way to the deepest recesses of the earth, then they are reservoirs of uncanny stillness, emblems of some interior serenity that we have yet to attain.

The gentleman revisors almost certainly failed to attain it. They concluded their work with a grim accounting of crimes and punishments worthy of an inquisitor's taste for suffering. I list the results in the section of my machine that follows hard upon its discussion of emancipation. They are the laws that bring "Laws" to a close. For high and for petty treason, the revisors recommend impoverishing the traitor's family as well as executing the guilty party and, in some cases, dissecting the corpse, presumably with the idea of displaying its severed head, torn limbs, and mangled torso in various places of public assembly to gratify the civic beast. A poisoner, upon conviction, dies by poison, but by the same deadly agent or by a different one, the revisors do not say. Some of these occult substances inflict terrible suffering before they kill, like King Hamlet's weeping sores or Hercules writhing in a coat of fire. Others put a victim gently to sleep, like the serpent's venom did the Queen of Egypt. I suspect our revisors were reluctant to go into much detail, sensing perhaps how a less vindictive future might be likely to view these barbaric judicial practices.

For rape and for sodomy, castration was the prescribed punishment, followed one assumes by a measure of public scorn verging on mockery, a refinement on justice that the perpetrators might have willingly traded for long imprisonment. But the revisors do not mention any additional feature of the sentence other than mutilation.

For crimes that result in maiming or disfigurement, they recommended retaliation in kind plus a monetary settlement on the victim, after which all parties go free to exhibit their scars and stumps among the people at large, perhaps as some form of savage deterrent. This portion of the perfected code seems to have emerged directly from Levitican law. My readers a hundred years hence are bound to wonder how such a crude appetite for retribution survived at all into a highly civilized age, unless civilization itself is in part simply a veneer. The emancipation amendment was a tissue of inconsistency at best, but it was far from brutal. That fact alone, perhaps, would not have doomed its chances for enactment, yet the revisors ultimately buried it in a bundle of over a hundred bills that languished for a decade or more in some clerk's drawer while the Revolution ran its course. Most of them never came up for debate.

All the brutality of the slave system, however, seems to have percolated through the revisors' gentlemanly brains and collected in a dungeon of grotesque mineral formations that conclude this remnant of the penal code. For a dozen common offenses and minor acts of larceny, they suggested various combinations of forced labor and steep fines, supplemented here and there by whipping, by ducking, or by exposure in the pillory. Witchcraft at least we appear to have outgrown, but perhaps not completely so, for the amended criminal code still took a dim view of pretensions to witchcraft and prescribed stripes to the pretenders, no doubt because a large proportion of the population remained vulnerable to superstitions as old as mankind. Even now in the dead of night, or in the depths of a mental cave, many people still believe in magic and fear its dark practitioners. In the enlightened view of the gentleman revisors, it is criminal to trade in fear.

Suicide with us remains a crime, as do apostacy and heresy, though we pity rather than punish them. They are punishments in themselves, as the testimony of the Arch-hypocrite has already made plain.

Schools

"A surgery, a guillotine, a map, and a lantern carried by three semi-enlightened guides into a dank mental cave. Have I left out some feature of your third drawing? The two Minotaurs you seem to overhear at the bottom of your sinuous descent? The fact that the key to your eye-draught turns out to be an elaborate monologue that your readers only encounter long after they have forgotten the cave map itself? Little wonder that my family and I were bewildered by your pages.

"Spiritual diseases of the kind that you hope to cure are far too subtle for a surgeon's crude remedies. The tumor that devoured my daughter taught my wife and myself a bitter lesson on the limits of their skill. You know my feelings about the guillotine—it is the child of fanaticism. Take your head off the block and burn the vile thing. Your eye-draught, however, I can decipher far better now than when I first encountered it in the *Notes*. My vision has lately grown so dim as to be almost useless, and I am forced to peg about house and farm with a stout cane. But I can manage to grope my way through your verbal cave, as long as my faithful secretary is willing to keep reading to me, much like you and your servant companion bending together over a scrap of paper and tracing your twisted route.

"Of all the images you invoke, the lantern is by far my favorite, the lantern and the guide that any descent into Hades requires. I have some doubts, though, about those enigmatic pools at the bottom of your cave. To my mind they resemble death more than life, stagnation rather than stillness. Hardly a serene destination. You once expressed some hope of finding or building a center of domestic calm amid the world's Heraclitan flux, a dream that you tried to realize on your mountaintop or in the compact octagons of your forest retreat. But we are streams and cannot cease to run. The current dwindles to a trickle over time. The channels get too shallow to navigate as age overtakes us, but the sound of movement, however faint, remains oddly comforting. You must have found it so even deep underground, listening to a steady trickle from the tips of the stalactites, building their delicate stone columns on the cave floor."

As you say, perhaps the pools are Stygian places after all. Virgil describes Cocytus as a seething whirlpool, but he dismisses the Styx as a mere swamp. Charon is forced to pole his way across the stagnant muck. But enough of this underworld excursion. I am ready to clamber out of the cave, brush the cobwebs from my hair, and follow the next set of breadcrumbs wherever they happen to lead.

At one point in the years after I first published my book, I pasted a long and rather silly note into the copy where I collected all the corrections I thought of making in some future edition. It was an elaborate description of the living body as a wind tunnel, inhaling atmospheric fluid and diffusing its caloric energy along the bloodstream, counteracting the chill of winter with the aid of fire, wool, fur, or feathers. Humboldt discovered certain downy leaves high in the Andes that his Indian porters used to make their beds, fending off Chimborazo's extreme cold. I was delighted with the information and stuck it in my note.

Vital air as a vehicle of heat was the *primum mobile* of life, as far as I was concerned. Without it, the heart muscle's irritable fibers would grow still, the blood slow to a stop, and the body revert to inanimate matter.

Why on earth I thought my reader needed a stern reminder to keep warm is a mystery to me now. The note gives the impression that I am entering my dotage. At best it is a pedantic exercise, but it does have the virtue of fixing one's attention on bodily diffusion and circulation, as if I were a fervent young tutor schooling my pupils in the latest physiological knowledge. A living body becomes a dead lump if it cannot draw in the free air, harness its volatile force, awaken the heart, and propel the blood through its channels. At least in so far as mere animal heat is concerned, we are the very streams you describe.

"The notion pleases you then, as a physical principle at least."

As a physical principle and a potent analogy. In the midst of all the gibbeting, ducking, and whipping that the gentlemen revisors dealt out, they also turned their attention to diffusing as much knowledge as possible though the mass of the people using a system of public schools that resemble the air-cells of the lungs. One of their bills proposed scattering hundreds of county school districts throughout the state. These would act like little pockets of vital oxygen covering a few square miles apiece, each furnished with a tutor able to teach reading, writing, and simple arithmetic to any child in the district whose parents saw fit to send them. After three years of free instruction, families might pay a fee for as many more years of schooling as they liked, probably for those pupils who seemed most eager and apt to learn and whose labor was not urgently needed tending crops or managing livestock. The revisors did not envision compulsory education any more than they envisioned laws to impose compulsory breathing.

Each year a supervising visitor would arrive in each district, examine the students, select the best genius from among the poorer boys, and send him forward to one of twenty grammar schools to be scattered around the state. These lucky few would then begin the study of Greek and Latin, along with geography and some of the higher branches of arithmetic, all at public expense as before. Families able to pay to send a son to grammar school were free to do so, provided the boys passed the visiting examiner's scrutiny. Your wife, I remember, was troubled that the plan made no provision for an ambitious girl with an appetite for books. But the revisors clung to their boy schools and their ancient languages in the hope of discouraging mental lethargy, a vice to which they felt boys might be peculiarly susceptible.

"A flabby excuse. It would not have satisfied my wife, but go on."

After two years of further study, the best student in each of the twenty grammar schools would be allowed to continue at his books for six more years, again at public expense. A family is less likely to balk at keeping a son from learning a useful trade if the opportunity for acquiring additional education costs them nothing. The residue of the grammar class would be dispersed to rejoin what my *Notes* term the rubbish of the general population. To the revisors it seemed pointless to give this aspect of their system a sugary cast. Their main intent was to educate a cadre of citizens fit to serve as guardians of the people's liberty. The idea steals a page from Plato, but it is one of the least objectionable of his foggy notions.

At the conclusion of six additional years of study, half of the advanced scholars are to be discontinued, some to teach in the county schools, perhaps, while others are left to their own devices, finding work as merchant clerks or apprentices. The other half enter college, studying languages, history, politics, rhetoric, natural philosophy, and all the useful sciences, for another three years, once again at public expense. They may or may not receive degrees. The revisors show little interest in such ceremonial details. Some students will no doubt pursue the law, some will turn to trade or medicine. A few will find work as tutors in great households up and down the coast. Others will find ways to squander their opportunities, running away to sea, or devoting themselves to drink. The revisors make no mention of preparing candidates for the clergy, though a few students will probably wind up in pulpits here and there.

> "So far so good, with the exception of your book's contemptuous reference to human rubbish. Surely the gentlemen revisors did not employ such inflammatory language in the bill that they prepared for their colleagues. The delegates would have broken out in a fury and rightly so. Why run the hazard of enraging readers in a machine that proposes to rescue them from their demons?"

I might reply simply by repeating that merit is a ruthless master, but the revisors had a more complicated idea in mind. Merit is as indiscriminate as she is ruthless, scattering talents among the poor as liberally as among the rich. The plan sets out to capture and cultivate mental gifts wherever they might be found and equip their possessors to manage the people's affairs. To some minds, words like *rubbish* or *residue* imply little more than the scorn that wealth and privilege have grown accustomed to visiting upon poverty. To the revisors, they hinted at the chasm dividing knowledge from ignorance. I invoke the demons of rank and birth in my pages in the interests of preparing for yet another mental avulsion, briefly placating our tinsel aristocracy in order to lay an axe to their roots.

Delegates from poorer constituencies in the state might indeed be the first to howl their objections to any educational act that seemed to consign their children to mediocrity, but the howling would quickly shift to the great landowners and merchants once they realized that their own offspring were just as likely to find themselves on the rubbish heap, if that is where their abilities and their character conspired to place them—more likely in fact, given the kind of habits they develop in their privileged cocoons.

"It is a risky tactic."

Well worth the risk if it awakens the pride and ambition of the poorer class of citizens and alarms the wealthy with a foretaste of their future.

"The schools, then, are your guillotine."

A comparison every bit as revolting as my reference to human rubbish. I am delighted to accept it.

The county districts may well be the humblest layer of our educational pyramid, but they are the very point at which the free air enters the body politic most deeply and penetrates to the lungs and the heart. Much will depend on the skill and the energy of their tutors. The particular conduct of the county classrooms played no part in the bill of revisal, but the gentlemen revisors agreed among themselves that these were the years in which the youngest students should have their memories stored with the histories of Greece, Rome, Europe, and America. The Bible and the prayer book might do for home instruction, but a public school is not a useful place for tromping out Samson's riddle and puzzling over fox tails. Works of history candidly disclose how the elements of individual morality can breed prosperity or misery for cities and nations, how happiness springs not from one's material condition in life but from just conduct and a good conscience. The lessons are too important to be entrusted to murky legends.

This earliest course of study will, in time, produce a people capable of discerning the wiles of ambition and thwarting its designs, of passing enlightened judgment when less reflective minds are mired in prejudice. It will make the public at large a safe repository for their rights and a formidable foe of those who might seek to undermine them. In short, the county schools are the soul of the revisors' system. A handful of the best geniuses filtering their way through some years of college cannot of themselves prevent the government from succumbing to human weakness. The people as a whole must, as far as possible, be made immune to corruption. Public libraries and public galleries must be furnished with works of art and generous collections of books, so that appetites and skills stirred by a handful of years in school can find an outlet during hours of leisure, and act as places where groups of citizens might congregate to consult the records of the past, study important natural curiosities, and view monuments to taste and beauty that the ages have produced.

"You realize, of course, that you are describing your mountaintop retreat."

Why shouldn't every citizen have access to such a retreat? The bill of revisal provides for public money to support galleries and libraries in our centers of population at first, perhaps, but eventually they too will be diffused through the state widely enough so that no one need endure an existence utterly devoid of spiritual resources.

"What about your churches?"

They are not sufficient.

"I suspect your clergy would quibble with that claim."

They are a profession of quibblers.

"Then let me propose a quibble of my own. Your gentlemen revisors seem to have envisioned a mode of public education aimed at vigilance rather than delight. True, they have set aside their interest in the pillory and the whip for the time being, but only in order to propose a system of schools that nurtures suspicion more than pleasure. Your public galleries seem at best an afterthought. By all means let us scatter several crates of statues and paintings through the countryside in order to give the folk something to gaze at when they are tired of the soul-killing spectacle of history, but let them above all be wary of corruption. This breath of free air seems not a little stifling to me. Your physiological footnote spoke of awakening the heart, of cultivating the sheer exultation of existence. Where is the heart in your plan?"

My fears of degeneracy may have gotten the best of me. Cunning and wickedness will forever busy themselves by adopting various disguises in order to betray the public trust. It would be foolish to let down our guard. Even so, our model for the future should draw more from Athens than from Sparta. Better yet, we should adopt no model at all other than the suggestions of our own good sense, founded on our highest ideals. Samson's riddle may be a good way of keeping little boys out of mischief while dinner is cooking, but its greater value lies in the lesson that power is best allied with sweetness rather than force.

The gentleman revisors intended to foster just such an alliance at both extremes of the educational pyramid.

When I was first preparing my book, the sole college in the state was capable of accommodating no more than a hundred students. Its namesake monarchs had endowed it with a considerable grant of land and the revenue from a tobacco duty, to which the colonial assembly added additional funds drawn from taxes on liquor, skins, and furs. Altogether it was a sordid basis for a seminary of learning, but in combination with some modest tuition charges, the annual income was sufficient to erect a handful of brick buildings and support five or six professors, fully half of whom were devoted to the study of divinity or the conversion of the Indians. The entire enterprise was a noble idea shot through and through with flaws. For one thing, its students were generally either children just beginning a study of Latin and Greek or young men with few aspirations beyond acquiring the rudiments of science and frequenting the local taverns.

As a gesture of respect, the college was granted a representative in the state assembly in recognition of its unique role in the life of the commonwealth. This feature of our colonial regime still startles me whenever I recall the partisan acrimony I observed in nearly every session of the Senate over which I presided during your Presidency.

> "A bag of snarling cats, as you and I have lately agreed. Had we thrown a hapless professor or two into their midst, the poor creature would never have survived."

I sometimes wonder. In any event, with the outbreak of Revolution the revisors were able to replace the preponderance of divinity professors in our college with a number of scholars equipped to teach law, anatomy, medicine, mathematics, moral philosophy, and the fine arts. In place of a curriculum revolving around Greek and Latin, the Board of Visitors substituted modern languages, and the laws of nature and of nations. In due course we hoped to add Anglo-Saxon to the curriculum. It proved impossible to uproot the professorship aimed at the conversion of Indian peoples, but the revisors envisioned turning its emphasis toward studying the customs and languages of the various tribes in the hope of tracing their connections with one another.

"By *revisors* you mean exclusively yourself, I presume."

Am I so transparent?

"I am afraid so."

Be that as it may. This institution is still our only college. Over the years we have turned its attention away from filling pulpits to filling minds. With luck our House of Delegates may soon agree to open the second university that my obelisk inscription mentions, though that remains to be seen. So far, we have not distinguished ourselves in the number or the beauty of our public institutions. Our capitol building is airy enough, but its parts are ill-proportioned. The Governor's palace is spacious but ugly. The college and the state hospital for lunatics are both in the old capitol and both resemble brick kilns.

The original bill of revisal for establishing the public schools included provisions for turning the county districts into wards of local government on a broad scale, with responsibilities for maintaining roads and bridges, for managing the militia, for overseeing elections, appointing juries, caring for the poor, and providing a police force to ensure public order. They would in short be small republics unto themselves, treating with their own inhabitants and with those of neighboring counties as parts of a league of equals, giving every citizen a voice on matters of public concern and a sphere of public action in which to serve, long after they had completed their years of free schooling and taken on the responsibilities of men and women. In this way, too, we thought the free air might continue to invigorate the civil body, making it even less likely that a single center of money or of intrigue could purchase the government wholesale, as has been the case for too long in most parts of Europe.

Instead of laying your quibble to rest, I may be on the point of inadvertently reviving it. "Be ever vigilant," Head advises. "Be open to the ephemeral beauty of the world," Heart replies. I am an empire in conflict with itself. My two sovereigns and I often enjoy some spirited quarrels.

ꕥ

"You owe me a final picture, I believe. At this point we have followed a breadcrumb trail through the first three of your exhibits, descending into your racial hell in the hope of glimpsing some termination to its reign and surfacing once more to survey your county wards, those little republics that you hope will be able to impose some measure of reason on your lunatic criminal code. If I were to guess at the nature of the final picture, I should say that it is the ground plan of your new university-in-waiting, or perhaps an architectural elevation of its central building, the domed rotunda where your books, your marble bust, and your articulated skeleton will eventually come to rest, once your heirs open your bedside drawer and consult your unsigned memorandum."

A respectable guess, but badly at fault, I am afraid.

"It has happened before."

The fourth drawing is in fact the little squiggle of rivers and creeks in the final and longest appendix of the *Notes*, itself a machine within a machine or an archive within an archive, ending with a simple image that most readers are prone to overlook altogether and that you have already declared to be too crude to play an influential role in my emancipatory scheme. I was immensely delighted when you brushed the sketch aside. The opportunity to startle an unsuspecting audience with some odd novelty or other is one of life's undervalued pleasures. My grandchildren and great-grandchildren are my customary foils, but I am happy to add you and your secretary to the list.

It is curious, however, that neither of you recognized the squiggle. It is actually a fragment of the engraved map that the two of you have spent so much time studying.

Take up the map once again and look for the tiny cross marking Braddock's Field near the site of Fort Pitt. Your secretary will have little difficulty finding the place if he has any feeling at all for recent history. Even the youngest students in our county schools are familiar with the story of the massacre. Braddock's scorn for his Indian scouts is nearly legendary, as is the role that Washington played in organizing the retreat. I expect you are as weary as I am of reading about his disregard for danger, the horses shot dead beneath him, the pitiful spectacle of English corpses in their vivid red coats littering the forest floor.

Too much of our past is polluted by such brutal scenes, a tangle of greed and grievances, rage and fear, all set in furious motion so that one European monarch or another might build an outpost at some convenient river junction where Indian trappers could exchange their pelts and their land for gunpowder, whiskey, and smallpox.

I apologize for this outburst. Where was I?

"You were directing us to Braddock's field on your map."

Oh yes.

Fold the engraving into a small square as neatly as you can, keeping Fort Pitt near the center, and then turn it ninety degrees counterclockwise as if you were pouring out the contents of a bucket. The fortieth parallel of latitude will now run off toward the top of the sheet. The Allegheny River will wend its way from left to right toward its junction with the Monongahela. The Ohio will twist down the center of the square to meet a little tributary called Yellow Creek just after it crosses the dotted line marking the Pennsylvania border.

Now that I have you thoroughly turned around, set the folded square aside for a moment and open my book to the last few pages of the fourth appendix, where the little river sketch appears. Place the sketch beside the square and compare one squiggle to another. You should now be able to see that the crude drawing you were so quick to dismiss is in fact a careful tracing of a segment from the map.

For simplicity's sake, I have left a few place names and a few creeks off of the tracing. Pittsburgh now stands where Fort Pitt once did. The line of longitude that bisects the squiggle marks five degrees west of Philadelphia, though west is now down and east is now up in my topsy-turvy version of the world. Yellow Creek takes on more prominence in the tracing now that its letters are right-side-up, though its name is innocuous enough. The appendix explains, in excruciating detail, that Yellow Creek, along with a portion of the bank of the Ohio opposite its mouth, was the site of another wilderness slaughter, much smaller in scale than the Braddock disaster but momentous enough in its own way.

My book tries to explain what happened there by making an elaborate collection of documents, reproducing a piece of my map, and gathering all the surviving records together in a pamphlet that appeared just as you and I were beginning our bitter electoral contest. The ultimate destination for the pamphlet was as a final appendix to my *Notes.*

> "A strange time to be taking affidavits and turning maps on their sides, if you don't mind my saying so. Though given the nature of your book's collecting mania, nothing should surprise me.
>
> "The election was bitter indeed. My wife took the political attacks far more personally than I did. She could not bring herself to believe that some of the slanders published on behalf of your candidacy met with your approval, but your silence on the matter wounded her. To her mind you were always the widowed father of our Paris years. She loved your daughters and loved you through them. No one has ever embodied more perfectly than she the second of the two sovereigns who divide your mental empire between them. The Heart I mean, in all its openness and susceptibility to suffering.
>
> "Given the nature of the times, I don't think either of us would have paid much attention to the new appendix in your book, though friends must surely have pointed the pamphlet out to us when it first appeared."

She wrote me, you know, when the newspapers reported that my younger daughter had died.

"She showed me the letters."

You had lost a son not many years earlier. For some reason I thought our mutual pain might help us put aside old political grievances, but she bristled when, like an idiot, my letters touched too soon on public matters.

I read books very well, but people very badly. Though if she and I had been meeting face to face, I hope I would have recognized the brewing storm in time to seek shelter.

"Had I known the two of you were corresponding, I could have warned you to tread carefully. Her sympathy for you as a parent only intensified the resentment with which she contemplated you as a politician. But by then you and I had long ceased exchanging confidences, and I doubt that you could have applied my tactical suggestions with any success. You never impressed me as much of a tactician."

An avid legal scholar often makes a poor lawyer.

"An accurate assessment. Yet despite your aversion to engaging in newspaper quarrels, you did occasionally display a combative flair in your personal correspondence. Now and then some unscrupulous editor would find himself in possession of one of your letters and publish it to the world without the slightest qualms. Much as I deplored these betrayals of trust, I did note with some satisfaction your gift for invective.

"Those were the disclosures that most troubled the members of my family. My son had come to consider you almost a second father when his mother and I left him in your care to go haggle with the Dutch bankers at the end of the war. Even the excruciating underworld journey in your book did not impair the esteem with which he always regarded you. But as he followed the tortuous course of our campaign from his post in Berlin, he was unable to excuse the momentary bursts of feeling your letters contained, however much he despised the editors who had printed them. Much like his mother, he was not given to emotional eruption and had difficulty understanding its pleasures. Whereas I am inclined to vent my feelings quite freely and tolerate in turn the spluttering outrage of others.

"Not that you were ever given to splutter. Quite the contrary. The more elaborate and the more balanced your sentences grew, the more impassioned you seemed. I often think of myself as so much loose powder fizzling away in an abundance of smoke and sparks, whereas you always reminded me of a tightly packed keg holding its energy in reserve until the time was ripe for one mighty detonation.

"Not even in the most acrimonious phases of the campaign, however, did I doubt your great abilities or your devotion to the country. The press was another matter. Editors relished mocking your *Notes* as the electoral contest grew near. Westerners despised you for your defense of Indian character; northerners for your slaves and for what they took to be your infidelity; and southerners for your emancipation dreams and your betrayal of the planter class. It proved only too easy to present you in caricature as the befuddled philosopher in his mountaintop observatory, forever fussing with his tables of plants and animals or his scientific apparatus, hunting up prodigious bones or moose carcasses for shipment to the Jardin des Plantes, taking barometric readings five times a day, weighing swine or squirrels, measuring Indian genitalia so as to refute Buffon's sexual insinuations and defend North American manhood. They took ample revenge for your cool dismissal of human rubbish."

The caricature is not entirely without merit.

"No caricature ever is."

The fascination with genitalia, however, was Buffon's, not mine. I quoted him in French to make the attribution as clear as I could, and kept my own words well within the bounds of decorum, but ever since Linnaeus began cataloguing the reproductive organs of plants, poets have been inclined to see a Turkish seraglio in every tulip. Add to that the occasional language tutor who took pleasure in translating Buffon's slanders for an appreciative tavern audience. I should not have been surprised that my opponent and I were soon tarred with the same brush.

"You do treat him rather tenderly."

What could I have gained by gibbeting him in the spirit of our criminal code?

"Very little, though the spectacle might have been interesting."

More to the point I agreed with at least one assumption that lay at the heart of his invidious delusions.

A long and affectionate contemplation of Ukrainian oxen had led our French friend to conclude that the far northern latitudes produced the largest quadrupeds on the globe; this despite his own familiarity with elephants and hippopotami thriving in torrid zones, to say nothing of the stuffed bison specimens that I had sent him. In time he recovered some of his senses. "To be sure," he concluded in his snug Parisian chambers, "the heat with which a passionate sun bathes a loving earth is the key to animal growth"—a reversal as dazzling as his original error. He then reasoned that America was neither hot enough nor cold enough, wet enough nor dry enough, to support the noblest animal specimens, men included.

The climate of the New World, he believed, diminished our natural ardor—a thoroughly French sentiment. Since our Indian peoples lacked the power of love, they remained stupidly inert when not motivated by hunger or fear, showing little interest in their families, their neighbors, or their fellow men.

"You compared these notions to the fables of Aesop, I believe."

It was a grave injustice to Aesop, for at least he did not pretend to be writing sober zoology. Buffon was in the grip of a mania. I should have consigned him to our lunatic hospital.

"A more humane decision than gibbeting. Your lofty civility quite on its own, however, made your French opponent seemed positively unhinged—though not entirely so, it would seem. With which of his assumptions did you finally agree?"

With the assumption that the family is the school of human affections, the center from which our fellow feeling radiates to take in all of humanity. Without the steady exercise of these affections in their most intimate setting, they would wither away entirely, leaving us little better than ingenious predators, devising weapons to compensate for our lack of horns and claws.

As a lifelong admirer of Samson's example, and the center of a loving family yourself, you cannot but agree. I am thinking less of the hive in the head of the lion than of Samson's determination to transgress against tribal prejudice and find a wife among the Philistines, as if by doing so he might strike a blow against ignorance itself, a feat more memorable than killing wild beasts with his bare hands or ripping the gates of a city from their hinges. Twice he tried to overcome this intangible enemy and twice he failed. The Philistine lords were so implacable in their hatred of Israel and their fear of Samson's strength that they burned to death one bride and suborned another in their determination to be rid of him. It has always seemed to me that Samson must have been aware of their plots. Three times he deceives Delilah, describing three ways in which an enemy might safely bind him. Three times she betrays him and three times he easily routs his foes when they thought to find him powerless.

But then, almost as if he were weary of the charade, he reveals the source of his strength and accepts the agony of his blindness.

Children generally take delight in the stealthy regrowth of Samson's magic hair and the punishment that he inflicts upon his captors, as if the biblical lesson were somehow tied to their own fondness for unruly locks and dread of a monthly scissoring. As one grows older, though, it becomes all too clear that the story is steeped in Samson's voiceless melancholy, in his recognition that even the ties of marriage could not blunt the hatred dividing Philistia and Israel. For all his enormous strength, he could not make them one people. In the end he seems to have welcomed his blindness as if it were the bitter solution to a final riddle.

"I would suspect you of coveting a pulpit of your own were it not for the fact that your reading of the lesson is too dark even for a New England sabbath. We prefer our sermons to emerge from the shadows by the end of a Sunday service and offer at least some glimpse of a hopeful prospect. Melancholy, so far as I know, is not yet one of the biblical graces. It is certainly no way to bolster a weary spirit or help the mind gather its forces in preparation for the week ahead."

Is my reading truly as dark as that? Then by all means let the congregation dismiss me in favor of a more congenial guide.

In bidding farewell to the worshippers, I would only observe that I have carefully avoided treating the darkest and perhaps most interesting moment in Samson's story: the one that takes place after the father of his Timnah bride sought to tempt him with her pretty younger sister, after he had unleashed the foxes to spread their fire, after the Philistines in their fury had burned Samson's wife alive. In the first throes of his grief, he lashed out at his persecutors with all the grim physical energy of which he was uniquely capable, smiting them hip and thigh the Bible says, as if to emphasize the visceral nature of his rage.

But once the spasm was over, Samson withdrew to a remote mountain cave, to the depths of his consciousness in effect. I am not sure the Bible records how long he stayed there, cut off from food and water in a desert, alone with the mix of sorrow and anger that must have made his existence nearly unbearable. The legend passes over this terrible period in silence, as most readers of the story do, as you undoubtedly did in your joyful boyish response to the suitor's irresistible riddle.

To my mind the image of Samson in the rock cave of Etam is the one episode of his extraordinary life that I should choose to paint, not a sensational rendering of the aroused warrior slaying armies with the jawbone of an ass or the blind prisoner on the point of demolishing Dagon's temple. Such moments will always have their advocates among lovers of action. But only a master of shadows could manage the subject that I propose, one of the great Dutch artists perhaps who understood how the soul in pain could tolerate only the faintest glimmering of hope, no more than a lantern glow on the cavern floor.

"Melancholy strikes me as an inadequate term for the mental state that you are trying to describe. It suggests a settled form of dreariness to which the mind passively submits, as if to an endless, sunless winter. I sense no passivity in your Samson—Despair may be closer to the mark. If we are to believe Spenser, Despair, too, is a cave-dweller, though perhaps altogether too comfortable in his grim surroundings, as if living so long in the darkness had brought him to relish the absence of light. That form of perversity, too, seems inconsistent with the dark painting that you propose."

The artist I have in mind would have to be able to capture in oil an inextinguishable intelligence confronting the ignorance and savagery that mar our species, slowly reconciling itself to the necessity of long struggle and painful sacrifice before such formidable opponents would relinquish their grip on the future. Misunderstandings and betrayals lie ahead for the central figure in the canvas, but his expression must be capable of hinting that he accepts their necessity. I admired the work of David when I lived in Paris and was even privileged to visit his studio when Trumbull introduced us, but David's heroic scenes are command performances, suitable to an opera stage. They are insufficiently acquainted with the cave for the painting that I have envisioned.

A blend of Rembrandt's luminous shadows with Caravaggio's faces might come close to meeting the challenge. Or a late portrait by Goya, perhaps, the Spaniard whose etchings Pinckney first described to me nearly three decades ago. Not one of his court commissions but some subject that the artist chose on his own, after deafness had shut him in the chambers of his mind, alone with the monsters that memory had placed there.

"Would such works be included among the inspiring collections that your gentleman revisors hoped to scatter about the state?"

We could never afford them.

Religion and Manners

> "I have long despaired of competing with your command of ancient languages, the modern sciences, or architecture. In our grasp of history, politics, or law, I considered us equals. But in biblical knowledge, I thought the advantage would surely lie with me and my New England upbringing. A Virginian, I told myself, would be utterly lost once outside the covers of *The Book of Common Prayer*. Your comments on Samson convince me now that I was mistaken."

Pose a question or two about Levitican sacrifices or Judaean dynastic squabbles and you will quickly discover my vast reservoirs of ignorance. Not to mention fine points of theology. I am appalled at your capacity to absorb entire shelves of such factitious drivel.

> "Theology became, for a time, the marbles and ninepins of my old age. I ransacked the Church Fathers in order to delight in their egregious follies. It was an old lawyer's failing.
>
> "But I am by no means disposed to laugh at the prospect of human nature's complete emancipation. An impossibility it may well prove to be, but the attempt is far from foolish. I am eager to hear the sermon you mean to preach on the significance of your fourth drawing. No sooner did we fold your map, arrange your book, and prepare to investigate that curious little image than we found ourselves back in a cave once more. The allure of such places is irresistible, it would seem. They are mirrors of the mind, as a looking glass reflects the body. But how on earth did we get from the mouth of Yellow Creek to Samson in the cleft of Etam?"

I think we began our detour with Buffon's genitalia or thereabouts.

My little tracing of creeks on the upper Ohio appeared in a pamphlet that coincided with our political schism. That coincidence in turn reminded you of the hard treatment that my book received in the public press during the course of the Presidential contest. If I remember correctly, though, the first attacks came years earlier and only grew more virulent with time, much as the clash between our parties did.

"You were from the outset an inviting target. What newspaper editor could resist portraying the leader of our wild republicans as a man obsessed with the best method of killing weevil eggs? Merchants north and south were enraged at your theory that a dependence on the whim of customers suffocates the germ of virtue, and merchants purchase a great deal of newspaper space. Then consider the picture you paint of planters teaching their impressionable children to persecute their slaves! You could hardly have been surprised at the reaction such passages provoked.

"Man is a vengeful animal as well as an imitative one."

Oh, that mine adversary had written a book!

"Job's lament is beside the point. He at least was surrounded by nominal comforters. Almost from the moment of publication your ingenious machine drew a crowd of jeering enemies from every point of the compass. The planter class might have had a bone or two to pick with you, but you never denied that you were one of them. When you descended into the bigot's cave, it was your own brain that you mined for its loathsome ore. Western settlers, who despised you for your defense of Indians, could hardly accuse you of dealing in romantic delusions. Savage life as you characterized it was savage enough, but many readers resented your implication that we are all, in essence, savages. You might have placated some of them by giving a fuller picture of the brutality of frontier war, but the fact remains that whites paid bounties for Indian scalps. Our red foes never saw these terrible trophies as articles of profit until we taught them to do so.

"If anything, your book reserves its romantic delusions for the picture it offers of our incorruptible tillers of the soil. Farmers in your pages become saintly pioneers, mysteriously blessed with virtues that commercial and urban life despoils. I know a lot of farmers whom I would never be tempted to compare to the chosen people of God."

An over-zealous claim, I admit, but even in writing it I expressed some doubt about the entire concept of a chosen people. Surely a spark of virtue has to survive in some class of human beings, if only to prevent the Creator from growing utterly exasperated with our behavior and extinguishing us like so many of my weevil eggs. Husbandry seemed to me the most likely class, if only because its name suggests the careful preservation of a precious trust. The inhabitants of cities, high and low alike, are steeped in extravagance and envy. Paris itself, for all its wealth and beauty, always impressed me as a nursery of mobs. Great ports and rich markets demand great fleets to supply and protect them. Our navies jostle with one another on the open seas, pirates and robbers alike, gadding about the planet for luxuries that would never have tempted us had we tended to our own soil, worked it with our own industry, kept a wary eye on the weather, and driven off the vermin that threaten a good harvest.

"Farmers are not entirely free of envy and a taste for good things. Cain, as I recall, was a tiller of the soil."

And the Lord explained to him in so many words that if he paid attention to his fields and tilled them well, he could expect a reward. But he was jealous of the preference God seemed to show for his brother's fat sheep, sizzling on the altar. It is an altogether unhappy story, the outcome of which is one brother dead, another in perpetual exile, marked as a wanderer, and a deity who seems to take more pleasure in cursing mankind than in creating it. Cain's offspring are the builders of cities, I might add.

"It is a good thing that you kept that last thought to yourself, then, instead of mentioning it in your book. Merchants as the fit tools of selfish ambition are one thing. Merchants as the legitimate heirs of Cain are quite another. You might have met a much hotter reception had you returned to America as the author of such an argument as that."

True believers are never so happy as when they have identified an infidel to persecute. I happened along at an opportune time. We had made peace with England, expelled the Tories from our midst, and the French had yet to supply the world with a new Antichrist to fear and loathe. Under the circumstances our sermons had grown bereft of villains and our preachers had begun to fall asleep in their pulpits. My book managed to arouse the slumbering enthusiasm of more than a few religious zealots on the Atlantic coast even without inflammatory references to Cain and his trading partners. Why it should have done so still puzzles me. Merchants and slave holders might object to a passage here or there, but with the exception of a handful of pages, the book is a mild enough account of the natural world, coupled with some useful observations on government and trade. I go out of my way to dilute any controversy my opinions might spark.

A cursory reader might pass through the book's pages without ever noticing that the complete emancipation of human nature was of the slightest interest to its author.

"You are being disingenuous, old friend, even perversely so. Did you expect to attract cursory readers?"

I suppose not, but neither did I expect to attract inquisitorial ones. The tables alone should have dampened their fervor.

The complete emancipation of human nature will remain an unattainable fantasy as long as we insist on trying to control the thoughts of others. Surely every thinking person must realize by now that belief, in and of itself, is innocuous. One deity or twenty, fish-tail idols or dog-headed ones, octopus goddesses or Hindu avatars with elephant trunks for noses—the whole menagerie of immortals ought to be invisible to the state as long as they make no attempt to seize the state for themselves. Their very existence is evidence enough that we are not the masters of our own minds. Why should we expect to exert such control in the first place? Why indeed should we want to? Is uniformity of belief at all desirable? Is it even natural? Nature delights in endless variety. Never only one species or one god where a profusion would do.

The kinds of men, it is true, are not so different from one another as are the kinds of birds or the kinds of plants, but their faces and their minds are more so. No two sets of eyes, noses, lips or ears are quite alike. No two voices are entirely identical. No two people entertain identical feelings or identical thoughts, however closely matched their external circumstances might seem to be. Why should our beliefs, then, take identical form?

I have given way to a minor tirade, perhaps, but the accusations of infidelity that you mention never ceased to trouble me. Surely anyone who so much as skimmed my book or who read the first few sentences of the Declaration of American Independence could see that the opposite was true. The strictures of deism, I might add, always struck me as rather cold. Could I be termed a philofidiest—a faith-lover, as the philosopher is a knowledge-lover?

> "Too flabby a coinage for my taste. Even the most generous convictions must have an edge to them somewhere. The mind is a cutting tool."

I am inclined to agree up to a point. Your comical Church Fathers and theologians certainly relished applying anatomical knives and analytic fire to the souls of their neighbors. For the last two millennia the profligacy of the imagination has disgraced itself most egregiously in the invention of its gods, coupled with their cadres of ecclesiastical police. Together these heavenly and earthly allies conspired to produce their greatest of miracles: the invention of money.

> "Yet another line of argument that would have added fuel to the fire in which many of our contemporaries longed to see you burn."

I can't see why the assertion would have caught anyone by surprise. The only time Christ loses his composure in the entire Testament is when he drives the money changers from the Temple.

Even he was exasperated by the sordid relationship. Banks and churches worked out the details of their lucrative collaboration millennia ago. Caesar was the chief priest of the Roman pantheon, as well as the embodiment of Roman law and Roman power. Within a handful of generations after Jesus, Christians had renewed the partnership with Constantine and his heirs. Walk into any of our republican banks in any seaboard city and you can sense the bond even in the architecture. To call them temples of finance is no metaphor. Columns of polished marble, lofty ceilings, rich inlays, rows of grated windows where worshippers and minor priests regularly confer over acts of confession and contrition. Or, should I say, over acts of deposit and withdrawal, over loans and promissory notes negotiated between soft-spoken clerks and their silken clients. The only details the picture lacks are smoking censers and chanting monks.

> "I am the last person to excuse the excesses of finance. In Mr. Madison's late war much of New England, to my considerable shame, would have been more than happy to sell its birthright in return for sheltering its investments and its trading ships under the tender wing of the English fleet, while the western and southern states assumed the burden of defending the republic on their own. But even the venal bankers of Boston or New York would have balked at your bold dismissal of the gods as mere inventions, their own every bit as dubious as those of Greece or Egypt. I can give you a specimen of their sentiments: 'To be sure, sir, we worship our milled and unmilled coin, our crusados, ducatoons, rixdollars, and moidores, not to mention the many lovely varieties of Arabian, Spanish, and British gold, stamped with their mystic symbols. No pagan ever loved his tutelary deities more. But consider the Commandments, sir! There is only one true God and he brooks no gods before him!' A great deal of posturing and gesticulating would accompany this pious declaration."

Pious indeed. The god of commerce loves a closed market where he alone sets the terms of trade. I am, of course, reluctant to assault the Commandments. I know you hold them in high regard.

"Along with the Sermon on the Mount. Though in recent years I have boiled my creed down even further, to a single admonition: be just and good. One can quibble over definitions, I suppose, but even Franklin would have admired my brevity."

On the basis of those four words, you and I could put an end to religious quibbling. What the God of Moses wrote on a pair of stone tablets with the tip of his finger and what fills the theological tomes you used to collect are the effusions of two very different spirits. By the time Calvin finishes his discourses on the attributes of the Deity, I am convinced that he has given his reader as apt a description of Satan as one could desire.

"You are a veritable burning spring of heresy."

Our Virginia criminal code obliges you to pity me.

"Pity is not a word that one hears with any frequency from the lips of the Grand Inquisitor. I wish that ducking and stripes had been the worst of the inflictions that my forebears had visited upon the witches or the Quakers who sometimes beset them."

A dread of witches fed upon ignorance. The example of the Quakers struck a very different nerve, one more closely linked to shame than fear. One would think our emigrant ancestors in flight from a history of persecution, hard-pressed by nature and by the near neighborhood of powerful Indian confederacies, would have shown a greater tolerance for the religious enthusiasts in their midst. Or at least a greater capacity for ignoring their presence, perhaps even for laughing at their excesses. The world has long since learned to laugh at witches, with their ridiculous paraphernalia of charms and potions, much as it tolerates the harmless pretense of fortune-tellers like Pinckney's old woman with her cup of bones. But the mystic authority of an inner light is far less susceptible to ridicule. Ecstatic visionaries make uneasy neighbors.

> "For devotees of silence, they could be surprisingly loud."

Our earliest laws strictly forbade those silent meetings. Anyone so much as giving shelter to a Quaker assembly was subject to fines or imprisonment, a provision that our government modeled on the harrying of Jesuits in Elizabeth's day. A shipmaster who carried a Quaker into a Virginia port could be jailed for doing so. The intent of these measures seemed to be to turn our entire population into spies and informants. Any Quaker that our magistrates could find would be summarily locked up until agreeing to leave the state. If after two infractions of the law they returned a third time, they could be hung. It is only by sheer luck that our history, too, is not tainted by the judicial murder of one or two of these enraptured people.

> "George Fox once strode barefoot through the butcher stalls of Lichfield on market day, soaking his feet in the blood of slaughtered livestock and crying out 'Woe to the bloody city of Lichfield!' at the top of his lungs."

Prudent of him to remove his shoes and stockings beforehand.

> "He left them tucked underneath a shrub outside of the city in the care of some puzzled rustics, after being seized with a vision of ancient Roman persecutions. The butchers and their customers must have been bemused by the performance. Our New England Quakers favored a more direct message. One of them would slip into some unsuspecting village church on the Sabbath, wait for the sermon to begin, and then rise up in the pew, point a trembling finger at the minister, and proclaim, *Thou art preaching a covenant of works! Thou art bereft of grace!* The service would come to a halt until some elders could wrestle the fellow out. On weekdays, a Quaker woman might appear in the village streets, stark naked in the dead of winter, and declare that she and her brethren had seen through our vile hypocrisy to the spiritual nakedness beneath."

The accusation of hypocrisy will always be unanswerable. It hardly requires such extreme measures to inflict its sting. A gap inevitably persists between what we profess and what we are. No natural bridge can span it.

"Yet fanatics of every stripe will offer to do so."

Their reassurance comes at a terrible cost. How many millions of innocent beings have died in agony over the centuries, so that some charismatic zealot or entrenched church might continue spinning webs of unintelligible dogma to entrap hapless human flies?

"France has lately taught us, of course, that even atheists become eager inquisitors. The monstrous discovery should have come as no surprise. Dogmatic negation is its own ruthless catechism."

I relish our points of complete agreement!

Compulsory negation is as intrinsically idiotic as the Trinity. The world will always remain a hopeless muddle of competing faiths, just as the money changers will always be puzzling over the muddle of moidores, crusados, rixdollars, and ducatoons that believers bring to the temple in the first place, hoping to purchase suitable items for sacrifice. Surely the memorable outburst of temper that Jesus displays is a parable in itself. Either everything is for sale or nothing is.

Doubt is a disquieting condition of the heart. Guilt is still worse. We go to great lengths to shield ourselves from these forms of mental anguish, just as we quarantine ships that might bring some terrible disease into our bustling harbors. I give the Quakers credit for exposing our deceitful complacency, for dispensing entirely with the order of priests and trusting in the oracle of conscience alone. It was, in fact, the oracle of conscience that I had hoped to awaken when I carried my readers to the bottom of Madison's Cave, bringing them face to face with their reflections in the dark mirror that I had made.

"So far at least they have not embraced the experience and thanked you for your efforts. They seem in fact to have largely mistaken your mirror for an inadvertent self-portrait, an exercise in narcissism gone badly awry—a dog returning to his vomit, so to speak. Take your pick."

I half-expected the effort to miscarry. A jeremiad against bigotry makes no converts among bigots and, in any event, I was in no position to deliver one. How else could I approach the subject except in a voice from the *Inferno*—Ugolino devouring his children perhaps, a reprobate at once puzzled and horrified by the spectacle of his own grim fate?

Sooner or later some receptive spirit is bound to venture into the underworld with me, moving slowly and quietly through the sentences that thread their way down each page, listening to the whispered exchanges between my two imaginary speakers. I expect no sudden realizations to occur, no road to Damascus moment—just an opening at the end of the descent, a fracture in the limestone wall, a chance to breathe.

"Woolman, I remember, often spoke of openings in his journal. I thought the word strange at the time. The book came out in Philadelphia the same year that Congress met in Carpenter's Hall. Apparently, he would wait for an inner opening of some kind before he thought himself authorized to speak in one of the Quaker meetings he visited, or to question one of the slaveholders he encountered on his travels."

Once he felt himself authorized, what happened next?

"Often nothing. Perhaps his openings closed too quickly, or he was at a loss for words."

That is the liability of an exquisite conscience. Orthodox believers are never at a loss for some platitude to thrust down your throat.

"We are back at the base of your obelisk once more, paying homage to your statute for religious freedom."

Homage is not the term I would have preferred, though perhaps my epitaph invites it. One does not usually commemorate one's failures on a gravestone. I am too subtle for my own good once more.

> "You are too subtle for me, at any rate. How can a statutory defense of religious freedom constitute a failure? Only within the last four or five years have the New England states begun to catch up with your courageous example. Indeed, Massachusetts still maintains a church establishment, though the recent liberation of the people of Connecticut may shame us into freeing ourselves."

The people of Connecticut may yet feel their religious liberty to be contingent on political whims. Nothing that I have read in their new constitution would pose an insurmountable barrier to persecution. It does not directly prohibit a church establishment. Even our Federal Constitution goes that far, at least, though in doing so it seems to constrain Congress alone, leaving the states entirely unfettered as to the defense or betrayal of their citizens' rights. Our legislators appear to have great difficulty in declaring, once and for all, that the operations of the mind fall outside their jurisdiction.

The failure that I allude to in my epitaph is twofold. First, that the statute I wrote on behalf of the gentleman revisors did not pass into law for ten full years, and only then because someone other than the Arch-hypocrite of Monticello presented it to the House. Not a failure in fact, perhaps, but a worrisome sign nonetheless. Only the spirit of the times and the spirit of a people still aglow with their newly-won independence brought the law into being. But times and spirits change. Ordinary citizens inevitably relapse into ordinary life. Urgency and vigilance dissipate.

Hence the second and far more consequential sense in which the statute falls short: it is a failure in that it is a statute at all, rather than a clause in our constitution.

I put it on the obelisk in the hope that at least a few pilgrims would consult all of the documents that I appended to my *Notes*. The Act for Religious Freedom was the third of these, but it was preceded by the draft of a fundamental constitution that would have made the Act unnecessary. Had the draft been adopted as I wrote it by a special convention, it would have provided for the gradual elimination of slavery as well. It was its own, self-contained emancipatory machine.

But the state convention never met. And even if it had, I doubt my draft would have survived the scrutiny of the delegates. The Act that my shipping label mentions with such apparent satisfaction was a stop-gap at best, almost a forlorn hope. A subsequent legislative assembly, a dozen years hence, might repeal or amend it, as they would have a perfect right to do, eliminating all of its safeguards. No mere legislative body can curtail the liberty of its successors. A statute is by necessity as mutable as water. The preamble I wrote tries to anchor the principle of religious freedom as firmly as possible by affirming the gross impiety of attempting to constrain the freedom of the mind in a fashion that Almighty God so pointedly refrained from doing. But a preamble is just so much inspiring noise.

The Act itself explicitly forbids the state to compel support for any church, to molest its citizens in any way on account of their faith, to interfere with the free profession of belief, or to limit the civil capacities of its citizens on grounds of religion.

> "You are making out the case against yourself. Where is the failure in this resounding assertion of our rights?"

As I said, inspiring noise. Would it surprise you to learn that the upper chamber of our legislature objected to the preamble most of all, sending it back twice for emendations to the House of Delegates, resulting in much ill-will and a few clumsy grammatical modifications? Some resented the omission of any reference to Scripture in the statute's text. Some wished to reserve the right to disqualify atheists from giving evidence in court or from serving on juries. Others feared the prospect of an unrestrained press, free to propagate any principle or opinion however crude or ill-disposed its tendencies might seem. In the absence of a coherent opposition, and with skillful management, the Act passed, but it was far from a unanimous vote.

And like any statute, it can be revisited by subsequent legislative bodies, its freedoms slowly eroded or its protections weakened by increments until they become meaningless. Cutting its title into a granite obelisk is, at best, an ironic gesture, one that I suspect only a handful of pilgrims will detect.

> "Will your *manes* be satisfied if that select handful ultimately prevail over the indifference of their peers, summon the necessary convention, and embed the terms of the act in a fundamental constitution?"

No.

My hope is that the occult influence of two pieces of coarse granite on a wooded hillside will make all of us better readers, better minds.

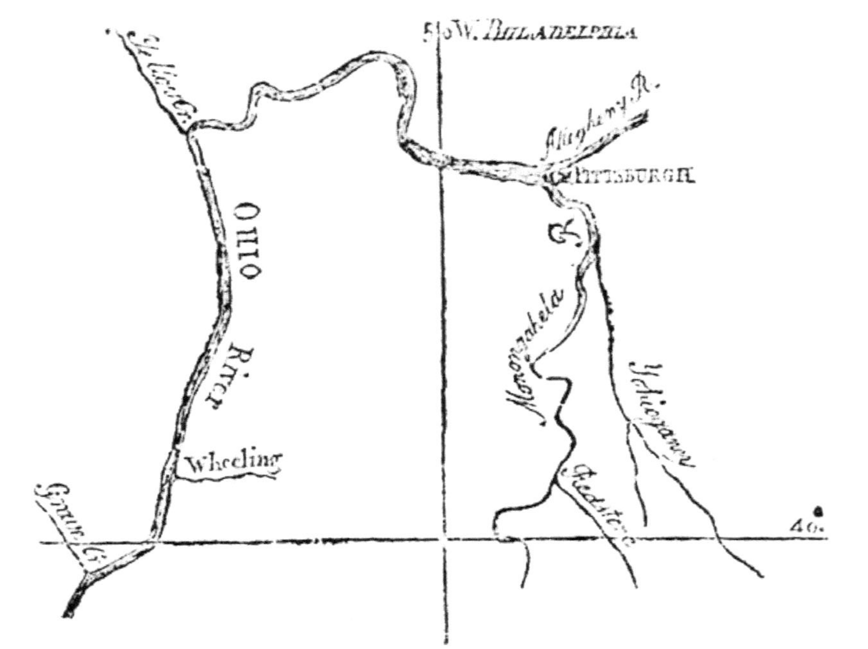
5° W. PHILADELPHIA
Allegheny R.
PITTSBURGH
Monongahela R.
Yohiogany
Redstone
40.
OHIO River
Wheeling
Green Cr.

Baker's Bottom

> "Your obelisk is now a study in irony, as well as a signpost directing pilgrims to the pages of a book that only a handful of them are even remotely equipped to appreciate."

As I say, too subtle for my own good. In any event, the bedside memorandum is hardly binding. My daughter may simply set it aside as a curiosity—too expensive to execute and too eccentric for the public eye.

> "Expensive and eccentric as a monument, perhaps, but not when you consider its role as a machine. A certain proportion of your visitors will no doubt chip away at your coarse stone and take home a fragment as a souvenir. They may not pay attention to the inscription at all, once they have recognized your name and begun to cast about for a tool with which to break off a sliver of rock to show their friends. One or two may be tempted to consider an act of ribald vandalism, but that is probably to be expected when even the tombs in Westminster Abbey suffer such indignities and Cromwell's desiccated head makes the rounds of English public houses. Your family will eventually have to consider a fence and a watchman, at least in good weather when tourists might be expected to visit.
>
> "Most pilgrims will wonder, at some point, why your high offices make no part of the epitaph, or your sponsorship of the Corps of Discovery to the mouth of the Columbia. But they won't wonder for long, I imagine, before heading back down the mountain to continue whatever journey they briefly interrupted in order to pay their respects at your grave. A select few, perhaps, will see the stone as a kind of syllabus, like the outline on the morals of Jesus that you prepared for Rush so long ago, only far briefer, more enigmatic. Oracular rather than prophetic might be one way to put it.
>
> "The four implacable faces of your tomb will act upon certain susceptible visitors something like your *manes* does when the invisible

plasma of its presence bathes your face. They will find themselves teasing out the words as they read them, rather than absorbing the epitaph at a glance on a section of smoothly polished marble. If your heirs have not yet built their protective fence, these careful souls may even surprise themselves by reaching out to touch the cool stone where the rock and the lettering blend together, running their fingers over the surface as they steep themselves in the influences of the place.

"The dimensions of the die and the placement of the lines on the obelisk will put the words at eye-level with most of your visitors, not at boot height like an ordinary churchyard slab, and not looming overhead like the inscription on an equestrian pedestal or at the feet of a bronze statue perched on a pillar. No one need crouch down or stand on tiptoe to decipher your message. You will meet your readers face to face."

If so, it will be more to their credit than my own, and I will do my level best to keep the ghostly encounter cordial but brief. The fate of Cromwell's head is positively appealing compared to the kind of reverential mauling that you have just described.

More to the point, I fail to see the connection to the syllabus. Rush and I spent many pleasant evenings together in the fall of '98 after the yellow fever had finished immolating a few thousand souls and burned itself out. For the sake of my daughters, I had fled the infection, but Rush stayed in the distracted capitol and did what he could to alleviate the general suffering. After I returned, the two of us had many lively arguments over the proper proportions of piety, courage, and fatalism necessary in the makeup of an ideal physician. One topic led to another and, before many nights had passed, we found ourselves sketching out the course of inquiry you mention. As I recall, Rush and I agreed that Jesus had purified Jewish deism and uprooted the ancient Stoics, replacing their cult of resignation with a scrutiny of the heart. The Stoics and the Deists are advocates of a numb endurance. Our preference was for a vigorous moral tribunal seated in the individual mind.

"Precisely where your epitaph seats it. Surely that is what our entire discussion up to this point has shown. In so far as you have led a life of action, it is missing from your gravestone. In so far as you have led a writer's life, you have turned inward toward the fountainhead of thought. I may have exaggerated the meditative state that your inscription elicits, but not by much. You must remember that we New Englanders are rather easily beguiled. Satan wormed his way into the minds of Salem Village through children's games. My ancestors read omens in the clouds and found a providential message in every sluggish garden snake that crossed their paths. The occult influences of your tomb are second nature to us. Now and then even I give way to the old superstitions."

I should never have tempted you by mentioning those uncanny encounters with my *manes*.

"Or that you tremble when you consider the prospect of God's justice rolling down like a mighty stream over your slave markets and plantations. Or that you fear a canker eating away at the heart of our national constitution. Or that you envision an apocalyptic convulsion taking place when our aroused fellow citizens rise up to strike off the last of their shackles. All these dire forecasts mentioned in your *Notes* are excellent themes for a fiery New Light sermon. At one or two points in your closing pages, you remind me of George Fox leaving his bloody footprints on the streets of Lichfield."

Fair enough.

"Perhaps you and I can visit your tomb on some Elysian holiday in the distant future and see how well your granite blocks are holding up under the reverential mauling you dread.

"Meanwhile I have been mulling over your reference to the last appendix as a machine within a machine. Its many moving parts are only too obvious: the letters, extracts, depositions, sworn certificates, and what-not that the pamphlet collects. One might even see the concluding squiggle of creeks and rivers as a slowly spinning wheel, tilting to the west and for all I know continuing full circle until north reappears once more at the top of the page and it begins a fresh rotation. Anyone who has ever tinkered with the spring in a pocket watch might credit your mechanistic analogy.

"Indeed, you have wound the mainspring tight at the beginning of the appendix where you lay out your intention to investigate, and

> if necessary correct, an injury to the memory of Michael Cresap that your book may have inadvertently inflicted.
>
> "But surely you could have accomplished that task with fewer pages. And having accomplished it, made any necessary changes in the book's earlier wording, reassigning blame where it properly belonged and exonerating the blameless. Instead, you go to great lengths to uncover an error, or perhaps a partial error, declare your intention to correct it, and then allow the original accusation against an innocent man to remain in the body of your book, where it can continue to inflame the feelings of an already vindictive group of readers."

And, apparently, where it can continue to puzzle even less vengeful minds such as your own.

"Exactly."

Your question, then, is why set out in search of truth, reach a verdict, and then deliberately appear to ignore it? And why do so when my candidacy for high office was at stake and my integrity was in question? Why break a lifelong prohibition against answering newspaper attacks by preparing an elaborate pamphlet that answers several at once?

Cresap's son-in-law in this instance kept peppering me with open letters in the Philadelphia and Baltimore papers, insisting that I produce evidence for an accusation that did not originate with me. It had appeared in the papers over ten years before the *Notes* were published. After I reprinted Logan's words in my book, they prompted no objection whatever through yet another ten years of schoolboy recitations and stage declamations until the end of the century approached, an election drew near, and a one-man volcano of resentment suddenly shook off his mysterious lethargy and rumbled to life.

Outraged innocence seldom lies dormant for a quarter of a century before declaring its grievances and demanding justice. Yet that is exactly the situation that my appendix attempts to confront. The innocence turned out to be partly real and partly not, but it took me several months to collect the documents, sift their contents, and unravel what seemed at first to be a simple case of mistaken identity.

By the time I was through organizing witness statements and sorting out facts, the case was far from simple.

My assailant's righteous indignation was clearly animated more by contempt for me and by political opportunism than by zeal to defend the honor of his family. Would such a tangle of motives cast a dubious light on the accuser and absolve the accused? When you come to think of it, which of us is which? Or were both of us both? This situation is just the kind of moral maze that my *manes* most relishes, the fine lines and deep shadows of a master etching.

It is a case study in the workings of unemancipated human nature.

> "I understand the reasons why you would resent such a belated attack on your defense of the Man of America. That a medley of small tribes scattered across a vast forest could, without the aid of a written language, nurture such eloquence as Logan displayed is a startling tribute to their genius. But the care with which you describe the initial reception of his speech, as well as the original sequence of events at Baker's Bottom, still leaves me with questions. The appendix omits almost as much as it includes. Four outbreaks of violence appear to overlap with one another, and all four gave rise to rumors that only make the confusion worse. Perhaps we can begin with the original wrong and work forward from there."

From Genesis then.

> "Not so original as that. The quarter century of dormancy interests me more. It coincides so perfectly with the opening stages of the Revolution that I cannot resist the tale. Bear with an old man for a moment.
>
> "The royal governor of Virginia had set out on his frontier war, vanquished a cluster of Ohio valley tribes, and extracted a moving statement from the Mingo leader whose surrender ended the conflict. Not a statement of remorse or even an acceptance of defeat. Logan simply dictated a handful of melancholy sentences to the Indian trader who was both his brother-in-law and his go-between with the English army. This morsel of native eloquence satisfied

his conquerors and caused a stir when its first versions reached Williamsburg, but I confess that I paid very little attention to it at the time, if I even took notice of its existence.

"My cousin and I had only recently arrived in Philadelphia to attend the Continental Congress, he on behalf of the Sons of Liberty, me as a somewhat less exalted delegate—the pugnacious Boston attorney who had managed to convince a jury to acquit the eight British soldiers charged with murder who had fired on an unruly mob a few years earlier. Our port was closed and our streets were filled with English regulars who occasionally prowled through the countryside, hoping to confiscate our militia's stores of gunpowder. Cool reason and blind fury were at loggerheads among us. I was trying to mediate between them in my own mind as well as among my fellow members of Congress.

"Meanwhile you had written a celebrated pamphlet defending the liberties of British America in language that even your friend Paine scarcely equaled. Yet in these same months you had also inherited thousands of acres and hundreds of enslaved souls from the estate of your father-in-law, including the children of his black mistress. No one in Carpenter's Hall at the time that you and Logan both rose to fame quite appreciated the depths of your dilemma, not until you came to Philadelphia yourself a year later. Most of the southern delegates and not a few of the northern ones owned slaves too, if not quite in such numbers as you, but none of them had stood before the court of public opinion and declared, in print, that flattery and fear were not American arts. None of them had accepted ownership of his wife's half-siblings, though the sexual excesses of southern planters were well known in certain northern circles.

"Your shadow-self as the Arch-hypocrite of an unholy republic took on life at that moment. It is hardly surprising, then, that you did not set all other affairs aside to determine the authenticity and accuracy of a speech by an obscure Cayuga warrior whose own eloquence had brought him both celebrity and disgrace."

I mention none of these private circumstances in my book's appendix. Nor did I touch on the political crisis unfolding at the time. To do so would only have been construed as special pleading on my part, and I was determined to make no concessions to my critics.

"Every reader of the appendix had lived through the crisis and could supply the context of your story for themselves. When the pamphlet

> first appeared, your American declaration was not yet twenty-five years old. Washington had been in his grave only a few months. The new constitution had been in place barely a decade. France and England were still at war. Indeed, war had become a way of life, off and on, from our far western frontiers to the channel ports of Europe for nearly half a century, most of my own lifetime in fact, leaving behind a train of reciprocal atrocities year after year until the mind despaired of counting the innocent victims, let alone bringing the perpetrators to justice."

Is that why you agreed to defend the English soldiers in court? To take hold of just a single instance of pointless bloodshed and try to unravel its causes? To bring at least one outbreak of twisted passions to the bar of fact and reason?

> "Since you put it that way, yes."

I remember reading your defense summation in Dixon's *Gazette.* Drunken jack tars, mulattoes, and renegades, you called the crowd on the Common, pelting a line of terrified British recruits with stones and bricks, bludgeoning one or two with clubs when they fell out of formation, howling "Kill them! Kill them!" until finally a handful of muskets discharged, five men died, and the newspapers cried "Massacre!" up and down the seacoast.

> "From the standpoint of an enterprising editor, there is always money to be made in a massacre."

Yes. And there was money to be made at Baker's Bottom from cheap rum and sharp dealing, or on the tributaries of the Ohio by slaughtering Indian hunters and stealing their furs, or in the forest near the Sioto towns, where the enraged Shawnee butchered a hapless Indian trader and scattered his head and limbs over the undergrowth by the side of the trail though he had nothing to do with the murders of Logan's family. Our Virginia and Maryland militia were never indifferent to profitable plunder. The Indians never ceased to resent the English practice of using liquor to their economic advantage. "Come and drink with us," the Big Knives at Baker's Bottom cajoled an encampment of Mingo hunters just across the Ohio. As many as a dozen obliged, men, women, and children. Within an hour all but one had been killed, most mutilated, all scalped, including Logan's brother, whose locks were decorated with silver ornaments that made the trophy all the more enticing to his killers. They spared only a little girl, the half-caste daughter of Logan's sister and her English husband. It is a savage story, made only more so by the rumor that the militia men, drunk with blood, tore an unborn child from the body of its mother and impaled the fetus on a pole.

"Can that be true?"

I wish for the honor of human nature that I could deny it out of hand. A white captive far down the Ohio heard the rumor from an old Mingo woman who had adopted him in place of a dead son. Or so he thought, for he and his new mother had to rely on signs to communicate. The Shawnee believed the account. They dismembered the poor trader as a signal that they meant to answer one barbarity with others. Shawnee mothers took to frightening their unruly children by whispering, "Cresap will get you," turning the Maryland militia leader whose memory I slandered into a demon owl. But why refrain from killing one child, only to butcher her pregnant mother before her eyes? The question alone is an index of our madness.

Logan was related by blood to the Conestoga Christian Indians who were massacred by Pennsylvania farmers and frontiersmen at the end of the old French War ten years earlier. The victims were old men for the most part, with a smattering of women and children, fourteen in all, their skulls split by tomahawks and in some cases their feet and hands severed as keepsakes by the settlers who destroyed them. All mild and merciful farmers, their minister later testified to the papers, exasperated to violence by the horror of Indian warfare, yet good church members in the main. He attributed their behavior to the infirmity of human nature.

Logan knew of this attack, yet in his speech he claims that at the time the atrocity did not trouble him. Why? Because he had imbibed a love of white civilization at its best, or of white rum at its worst? Either or both of these reasons earned him the contempt of some of his fellow Mingo hunters. They mocked him as they passed his cabin.

Did he choose to overlook the Conestoga killings because the victims had embraced the Moravians and betrayed their own traditions? Because none of them belonged to his immediate family? Because they were Susquehanna, rather than Cayuga, Oneida, or Shawnee? My brief pamphlet could only address so many questions. Michael Cresap's relations demanded I exonerate him of any responsibility for the murders at Baker's Bottom, and so I did. But at the same time the documents I collected implicated him in two other bloody assaults that laid the groundwork for that attack. When Logan accuses Cresap of murder, then, is he entirely wrong? No. Is the accusation based on misinformation? Yes. Did the massacre, in fact, leave him utterly alone, extinguishing his entire family as he claimed? No, for at least one niece survived and was safely returned to her English father. Other relatives had wisely declined to join the drinking party at Josiah Baker's tavern.

A reader of the appendix can easily piece together these circumstances from the records I supply, with or without the help of the numerical key I use to keep several different massacres from running together. They are each, in a way, tributary streams of blood flowing into a single ruthless river. Perhaps that is one reason why I tilted the map ninety degrees to the west. If I had thought to do so, and if the printer had agreed, I might have asked that the Ohio be rendered as a thick ribbon of red ink spilling down the page, with secondary veins identifying Yellow Creek, Grave Creek, and Wheeling Creek, where the preliminary murders took place, turning the landscape into a surgical diagram, laid open by two deep incisions that slice at keen right angles through the exposed flesh. I put no numbers on the map other than those of latitude and longitude. The reader who merely thumbs through the documents might be puzzled by its appearance. Red ink would help.

> "Anatomical knives and analytic fires once more."

Precisely. When I first heard Logan's words, I was struck by their emotional force. All of Williamsburg was. Who could overlook the obvious ways in which his plight mirrored our own, an advocate for peace exasperated by irrational violence, just as your colleagues in Carpenter's Hall felt themselves to be, a spirit immune to fear but overwhelmed by loss? The bonds of blood that tied him to his fellow man had all been cruelly cut, he said. Perhaps that was the image that first suggested to me the arterial streams of my sketch.

Only much later, as I transcribed Logan's words in my book, did I feel a personal tie to his loneliness: after the deaths of my own wife and infant daughters, after the accusations of cowardice in office had wounded me, after my own consideration of suicide. "He will not turn on his heel to save his life," Logan said of himself. Is that statement an assertion of courage, of despair, or of both? Surely both, my *manes* and I insist. Just such an abyss of feeling made his words irresistible to professional actors and schoolboy orators alike. Logan spoke to me in particular as from the depths of a cave, though I did not know it at the time.

> "Perhaps that peculiar intimation encouraged you to reprint his entire speech a second time at the end of the appendix, as stubborn a gesture as the four faces of your obelisk repeating the same epitaph to the cardinal points of the compass. You almost seem to be taunting your enemies, much as Logan did."

The gesture is not meant as a taunt. It is more a reminder to friend and enemy alike that the records I collect in the pamphlet begin and end in the mouths of speakers, starting with the Williamsburg gentry savoring a handful of remarkable sentences retrieved from a bloody frontier war. I can't even recall the name of the person from whom I first heard Logan's words, jotting them down in my memorandum book as I listened. It could have been any one of my acquaintances. We were all performing the speech for one another just as schoolboys and acting troupes would do for the next thirty years.

John Heckewelder wrote me a long letter detailing the particulars of Logan's life, the celebrated Oneida father to whom Logan always compared himself, his struggle with liquor, his descent into despair, and his eventual murder. I added it to the pamphlet. When I read it now, I hear a faint echo of the high Dutch accent that three decades of missionary work in the Ohio wilderness never quite eradicated from Heckewelder's gentle voice. I imagine I can detect the bland, official drone of the various court officers and notaries who took witness statements on my behalf and sent them to me, identifying themselves and vouching for the integrity of their sources. One of the murderers at Baker's Bottom apparently called himself "Edward King," perhaps in mockery of Milton's beloved friend. Who was he? My informant doesn't really know for sure. A renegade English officer perhaps, well-educated enough to know "Lycidas" but savage enough to admire a fine Mingo scalp. Did he speak with the accent of a British gentleman? We will never know.

The pamphlet documents seem to parade past my eyes and ears like a strange pageant, each speaker identifying himself and giving his testimony, filling in some fresh detail, confirming or confusing the accounts of others.

> "Then is your appendix a mechanism or a dream vision, a cleverly constructed device or a kind of hallucination?"

Do I need to choose? Consider it a specimen of our semi-emancipated nature and leave it at that. Logan loved the English, even as he glutted his vengeance at their expense. And though he never embraced some missionary creed, he knew the Bible well enough to mimic the final verses of Matthew 25 in the opening words of his speech.

> "I noted the allusion."

He never lived among the whites, as he said that he once hoped to do. But his sister married an English trader who accompanied Dunmore's army, helped negotiate the Shawnee capitulation at the end of the war, and later became a militia general and a judge. Logan's white brother-in-law even tried to explain to him that Michael Cresap was not directly responsible for the horrors at Baker's Bottom, though Logan clearly did not believe him. Perhaps he was already blinded by sorrow or had begun the course of drinking that would destroy his character and lead some of his own people to waylay him in the woods a few years later.

Despite his brother-in-law's efforts he may have remained satisfied that Cresap's example had emboldened others to massacre his family. Perhaps he had even heard the rumor that Cresap had accepted his brother's bloody scalp as a gift from one of the Baker's Bottom killers. Once Logan had made up his mind, he would not turn on his heel. In some ways he reminds me of Samson in his determination to unite himself to an alien people—Samson in his despair and in his intelligence.

"We can never get past the Nazirite, it would seem."

No more than we can get past the fratricidal passions of Genesis, the terrors of Revelation, the simple grandeur of the Great Commandment, or Paul's affirmation to the arrogant Athenians that all mankind are of one blood, throughout the nations of the earth. Sometimes I think it may have been in the spirit of Samson that my bedside memorandum compared the coarse stone of my tomb to the columns of my house—as if in death I, too, might grasp its supporting pillars in my hands and bring down the roof before its burdens could crush my grandchildren and my great grandchildren.

"You are thinking of the debts you left behind."

I am thinking of less tangible burdens than those.

The Cave

"I am afraid that some of my original confusion persists.

"You set out to explain to me why you would conduct an elaborate inquiry into the accuracy of Logan's speech, accumulate a thick bundle of sworn documents, reach a verdict, and yet neglect to correct the language in your book that aroused the resentment of Michael Cresap's family in the first place. Why go to such lengths after the lapse of a quarter of a century only to stop short of completing the task that you had set for yourself? The newspaper attacks were provoking, of course, but you had endured worse in the decade since your return from Paris with a tincture of Jacobinism clinging to your name. And worse still would follow after the election when, as my wife once reminded you, the viper that you had nourished in your bosom turned on you and bit your hand.

"Yet to those envenomed assaults you have never once replied. Only the challenge to Logan's credibility, and to your own, prompted you to step into a newspaper quarrel, not directly perhaps, but all the same. Your pamphlet amounted to a gazette in its own right, circulating in the streets of Philadelphia and Baltimore for nearly a year before reappearing as an appendix to your book."

Your wife's keen remark still stings. I re-read her letter from time to time, not out of any lingering regret but to remind myself of the quality of her mind and the dignity of her style. I seem to hear her voice too as clearly as I hear yours when I look at her hand on the page. She would have made a more potent New Light preacher than either of us.

"You and she were in correspondence only a few weeks after Burr had shot Hamilton. I suppose vipers were much on her mind."

She wasn't thinking of Burr. The venom in question was the public insinuation, from the pen of a party hack whom I had once patronized, that I had for years kept a slave mistress, my dead wife's half-sister—you met her as a girl in Paris when she was taking care of my younger daughter. That I had a second family by my concubine whose physical resemblance to me sometimes startled the visitors who came to my sequestered mountaintop, not realizing that it was the pleasure palace of the Arch-hypocrite. A rather clumsy Arch-hypocrite, it seems, who took no steps to keep his mixed-race offspring safely out of sight when influential guests were expected. Or perhaps no Arch-hypocrite at all, since he never tried to conceal what most thinking people took for granted as the sexual practices of all southern slave-holders. The response to such disclosures is not difficult to imagine.

"The man is no better than a Turk after all. No doubt he keeps a harem of slave girls at the ready, summoning them to his bed at whim. It is tantamount to rape, with the added incentive that the products of his loins are as vendible as the output of his nail factory or the corn and tobacco that he grows. You didn't know that the Great Agrarian ran a nail factory? Oh, yes. He is a Birmingham workhouse foreman in a gentleman farmer's disguise, squeezing profits from a shop full of malnourished boys. People say you can hear the clink of hammers all hours of the day when you approach the house. An overseer keeps an eye on the boys to see that the work goes forward at a satisfactory pace. Most of them barefoot no doubt and most with just a coarse shirt to cover their nakedness. Small hands and fingers are ideal for cutting sharp tips and flattening nail heads. The overseer whips any child who misbehaves. So I have heard."

My corn and tobacco fields have never yielded so abundant a crop as my life has yielded scandal to gratify the public appetite. When I called myself the Father of the University of Virginia in my grandiose shipping label, I as much as invited the ribald vandals whom you mentioned to deface my grave with less abstract attributions of paternity, most of which, so the thinking goes, I strenuously tried to conceal.

The Logan controversy stirred the embers of lurid innuendo, not that they needed much stirring. To many it seemed a matter of course that I would defend the reputation of a savage at the expense of an honorable Maryland family whose members had long served in the state's militia. I was, after all, a well-known connoisseur of savage flesh and a rank sexual predator, no stranger to the propagation of half-caste children—more a notorious libertine than a lover of liberty. Such a man should in any event be denied the suffrage of his fellow citizens. To place him at the head of the republic would be a sham. So the argument ran, not overtly but in the shadows. My pamphlet entered into the shadows to make its reply.

"How do you mean?"

Perhaps you need to trim your lantern more carefully or insert a fresh candle that can penetrate the cave's deeper chambers. I have turned the appendix into a kind of spinning dial, as you put it, precisely so that readers will find it necessary to grope their way through the documents and the details over and over again rather than settling for one quick and cursory visit. The appendix may well omit more than it includes, but it does so in order to pose more questions than it answers.

"Why, after taking such pains, does he fail to correct his original account of the atrocity? On second thought why should he? Is it so easy to distinguish the guilty from the innocent in this brutal story? Could we, in fact, have missed his pamphlet's larger point? Missed an altogether more intriguing claim that explains why he has bothered to revisit these long-ago events in the first place?"

You noted that the unpolished stone of my obelisk will make its inscription more difficult to absorb than if the words had been incised into a marble slab as smooth as a sheet of paper. And yet, the difficulty itself will make absorption all the more likely an outcome for those who take the trouble to draw close, perhaps even to touch the edges of the words. The appendix has a similar effect. It is a labor-making device, a machine that slows down rather than accelerates, asking a reflective reader to confront the many entanglements of fact and rumor imbedded in its darker passages.

Twenty-five years of death and dispersal had not made the circumstances surrounding Logan's speech as utterly irrecoverable as if they had been a heap of mammoth tusks or the jumbled contents of an ancient burial mound. I found it easy enough to sift ignorance from error at least with respect to his mistaken accusation. Within a few months of the first charge of slander leveled at my book, I had in hand a document or two from key witnesses testifying under oath, that would have given an adequate rejoinder to my critics, both on the score of the speech's accuracy and the culpability of Michael Cresap. But I wanted to re-create the atmosphere of rage and confusion that accompanied the murderous events, to expose precisely what the infirmity of human nature is capable of accommodating when it transforms otherwise merciful farmers into butchers inflamed by drink.

When did the cycle of provocation that led to Baker's Bottom ultimately begin? With an unprovoked attack on a party of Shawnee hunters that probably never occurred? When Logan's brother, fuddled with rum, tried to leave Joshua Baker's tavern wearing a white man's coat? When two canoes filled with armed and painted warriors set out from across the Ohio to ambush a party of Maryland militia men, as a friendly squaw had warned the whites might happen when they reconnoitered the Mingo camp the day before?

Or did the entire ruthless sequence actually have its origins in the pasture where Cain slew his brother?

My shadow-self as the great Arch-hypocrite presumes that hypocrisy itself is pervasive, that it is our nature to hide behind a carefully woven fabric of appearances, an elaborate costume that allows us to appear as one thing while actually being another. The Arch-hypocrite merely serves as the exemplar of a universal human trait, reason enough for our imminent extermination whenever the Sovereign Disposer should tire of the pathetic charade.

And yet what if the charade is not a complete fabrication? What if we are self-deceived as much as we are deceivers? Masters at the art of using one truth to blind ourselves to another? At crying "massacre" in order to obscure our own culpability? At finding scapegoats against whom to direct our furious indignation, as Logan did with Michael Cresap, as the Paxton mob did with the Moravian Indians they slaughtered, as the Shawnee did when they dismembered the first white man they met in the forest, as my enemies do when they sneer at the so-called self-evident truths that we proclaim from our slave auction blocks, or when they choose to gloat over the mixed-race children living on my mountain or the boys who cut nails in my workshop.

We are guilty enough, in all conscience, but we are innocent as well. Or perhaps I should say only that I know myself to be both things at once, to be the right man and the wrong man at the same time, just as Michael Cresap proved to be.

Long before I took up any of the high offices that my shipping label neglects, I spent a long afternoon deep in the cool recesses of Madison's Cave with my wife's half-brother as a companion in the darkness. Half-uncle to my orphaned daughters, the second or third child of my father-in-law's slave mistress, who joined my family as a boy just as the Revolution began. Together we prepared our eye-draught charting the invisible passages and chambers surrounding us, wondering what lay beyond the motionless black pools that receded before us into the shadows. Were they gateways to the future or to the past? Were they ends or beginnings? And which were we? I had only recently turned away from suicide and taken steps to re-establish my ties to life. He would ultimately take the opposite course, surrendering to drink and despair in a Baltimore tavern not long after my appendix had appeared and only a handful of months before the viper whom your wife mentioned sank his fangs into my hand.

Our eyes caught the glow of our lanterns as we threaded our way through the limestone teeth that filled the cave's narrow channels. It was much like descending through the skeleton of an extinct creature. Every few minutes we stopped to compare our impressions and add to our map, our two reflections peering back at us from the quiet basons we found at the deepest points of the journey. Odd, almost ceremonial bodies of water, as if they were waiting for the return of some mysterious celebrants whose arrival had been delayed while the stalactites slowly germinated and grew up from the cave's floor. At the time my young companion was not quite half my age, yet he had already lived half his life. When I think of him now, I think of Logan and of myself, three minds in the grip of a mute sadness that only one survived, three faces of a single stone.

> "Then whose would be the fourth face? The one that completes the cycle on the last surface of the obelisk?"

My own again, I suppose. The lone survivor looking into the mirror in search of his shadow selves. Or yours perhaps as the Arch-hypocrite's loyal arch-reader. But more than likely it is the face of the Anacreontic bard whose uncanny breath briefly touches my daughter's cheek before he disappears and leaves no name.

ꟷ

> "We are back at your eye-draught once more, I see, with its serpentine curves and curious arrows propelling themselves through the underground passageways like little bateaux hunting for a safe channel in a turbid river. I realize that they are meant to signal elevation changes, rising or falling on the way to a pair of breaks in the outline where water apparently blocks the explorer's way, but even that is a conclusion that your reader must infer from the drawing alone, since it contains no labels or numbers.
>
> "You omit both from your book as scrupulously as you omit virtually your entire political career from your epitaph—but for different reasons, I suspect.
>
> "The Heraclitan riddle at least is clear. As far as your eye-draught is concerned, the pathway up and the pathway down are difficult to tell apart. The remaining Greek fragments even assure us that the two figurative journeys are in fact the same, an insight likely to gratify the whimsical predisposition of your *manes*. Some of the riddle's pertinence to the events at Baker's Bottom is equally clear. The way down to the scene of the atrocity is the way up toward Logan's speech. To arrive at such poetic heights, we wade through

dust and blood. To affirm Michael Cresap's innocence is also to convict him indirectly of inciting grave crimes, a paradox that mirrors your own predicament so closely as to suggest that his face, too, might be said to gaze quietly back at you from one of the basons in Madison's Cave."

A reasonable enough deduction, since he and I share the distinction of having escaped blame for the crimes that we have actually committed while being slandered for the ones that we have not. It is hardly the outcome that I expected when I began assembling the pamphlet, but as my collection of documents grew, so did my uncanny bond with the man I was supposed to either condemn or exonerate, as well as with the man who first accused him. The weird reverberation seized hold of my mind, carrying me back to a crowded chamber somewhere in Williamsburg long ago, where I was feverishly scribbling down words as I heard them from the lips of a person whose face I can't remember. A testament of despair from a man whose face I would never see, however profoundly I came to share his feelings, and whose fate seemed to foretell that of a young man whose features I could never forget, illuminated by speckled candlelight as we listened to the echoes that filled the Sounding Room of Madison's Cave.

Perhaps as you have hinted, I am simply in the grip of an elaborate hallucination. Perhaps we both are.

"That is the atheist's glib recourse. I cannot take it seriously. Your little sketch, though, has risen in my esteem. I have just this moment set it side by side with the eye-draught, just as you instructed my secretary and me to set the tracing beside a folded section of your large map in order to see where the squiggles came from.

"My second pairing is more intriguing than the first, largely because you labelled and numbered the main features of the little tracing, just as you numbered the different murders that the appendix investigates for use as reference points in the pamphlet's maze of documents. The eye-draught, however, dispenses with reference points almost completely. It teases us with arrows for which it provides no key. I can hardly escape the conclusion that the tracing deliberately supplies what the eye-draught deliberately withholds, that the two images are inverse partners, like certainty and uncertainty, faith and doubt, knowledge and ignorance.

"You assured me when we began this discussion that after you had explained the little exhibit you were sending me, I would come to see all four of the drawings as variations of one another, as one image in four costumes perhaps. I suspect this inverse similarity is part of what you meant me to discern.

"On a whim I decided to rotate the third of the four exhibits, much as you did the final one. In the case of the cave, I elected to turn the image ninety degrees to the east rather than to the west, since its opening is high on the north face of the Blue Ridge. When you and your daughter's young uncle left her safely behind and set out on your underworld expedition, you must have turned southeast to climb the mountain's steep face, light your lanterns, and begin your descent."

Then you turned the drawing so that the cave entrance faced in what would be a westerly direction, if the eye-draught were a compass?

"I did."

And what if anything did you discover? I hope you are not about to propose more red ink for my harried printer to apply. I already anticipate strenuous objections to the tiny fleck of color I am trying to convince him to add to my tracing.

"Red ink would only confuse the issue. Once my first quarter-turn is complete, the eye-draught resembles a fragment from an animal's skull, with one or two knobby vertebrae still attached to its base and portions of an open jaw gaping to the right. I have seen the remains of beached whales or jaws of sharks that your sketch very nearly mimics, with no cranial cavity or eye sockets visible at all, only the bleached ridges of bone that formed the lower portion of the creature's head. If I didn't know better, I would have said that you and your young companion had stumbled into an ancient ossuary, an underground version of Big Bone Lick where some great antediluvian predator had come to rest."

Out of the eater came something to eat, or at least some rare fossil that I could retrieve for a curiosity and add to the antlers, painted skins, and mammoth bones that clutter the entry to my mountain-top house. When I repeated your experiment, in fact, the eye-draught actually took on a rather antlerish appearance.

For the last half-hour I have amused myself by spinning a copy of my book round and round on my reading desk until I began to grow slightly dizzy with the exercise. The jaws that you perceive are certainly formidable, if largely toothless. What would you say to the talons of an owl? Or perhaps half of a pelvic arch broken down by decay, as we might expect to be the case with an antediluvian monster? Or the wing bone of a bat still knit to the sternum but with its silky flap of skin long since decayed? The cave was carpeted with bat droppings when my companion and I explored it, though the vault was so high in many places that neither of us could see where the tiny creatures were roosting. We left well before sunset or we might have watched them emerge to begin their nightly hunt. Out of the eater came yet more eaters in a great flock, like the Spaniard's gruesome etching of the sleep of reason with its cloud of ferocious-looking bats circling the sleeper's cradled head. He too must have known something of caves.

> "Since you have taken up playing with your book, you must have noticed that as you continue turning the volume in a clockwise direction the eye-draught transmutes still further into a bony forefinger and thumb, pointing downward from a skeletal wrist toward the earth. After rotating another ninety degrees and it takes on the appearance of Samson's jawbone or, perhaps, of a sickle blade sweeping through a wet meadow. No matter how one turns the image, it only appears to have gloomy hints to offer a susceptible imagination. I prefer my tiny bateaux, trying first one passage, then another, in search of a navigable escape."

We can agree, at least, that the drawing is a kind of snare. Any thoughtful reader is bound to pause and wonder why that picture appears in the book and not some other, more obviously appealing one. I could have commissioned the young artist who was so taken with my grizzled locks and Russian coat to ride south with me for a day or two, on a final journey to my forest retreat, and make a sketch of the Natural Bridge along the way. I have labeled both locations on my engraving should a reader wish to make the trip. Any number of enterprising travelers passing through Philadelphia or Washington en route to our medicinal springs might have hired a talented companion and provided me with a pencil sketch of the Shenandoah's junction with the Potomac. Either image might have made it easier for an impressionable mind to share my wonder at those memorable places, but such pictures often stifle rather than stimulate the inward eye.

The silhouette of Madison's Cave has the opposite effect. The inward eye is, quite literally, the only organ capable of seeing it. Once it awakens and begins to take in its surroundings, even your little bateaux come strangely to life, blundering into one another as they attempt first one passage and then another on their restless journeys, none of them finding their way back to the cave's entrance, none of them passing through the gaps in the outline toward some unknown future. They seem trapped in a maze from which none of them is capable of escaping, though the opportunities to do so are at hand, ill-defined though the outcome might be. I sometimes think of them as little argosies of thought or tiny spermatic voyagers, vehicles of our complete emancipation perhaps. But what might that destination entail? Where might it lead? To repletion or to emptiness? To untrammeled genius or a benign imbecility?

"Our old comrade in arms Charles Thomson has drifted into the backwaters of imbecility."

So I have heard. Friends tell me that he has difficulty recalling his name or recognizing the family members who care for him, though he is as cheerful as ever and agile as a grasshopper. I will never forget the pains he took over a private printing of my *Notes*, supplying me with an appendix that reinforced my defense of Indian character in the strongest terms just at the point when my pages were about to face the public. Not long after that, I believe, he left Congress to raise bees and study Hebrew. Apparently if you sit with him now for any length of time, he will end up telling you the same story several times over with undiminished delight. It is the life of a cabbage.

"Cabbages don't tell stories, and I strongly suspect that they lack all capacity for delight. In some ways I envy Thomson his grasshoppery nature, if not his regrettable forgetfulness. At times I can still manage a three-mile walk over a rugged field or a rocky hill—it is slow going with a stout walking stick. But I am now completely unable to mount a horse. At other times, when a grandchild or my secretary finishes reading to me, I find that I can barely get out of my chair. Imbecility may not be the worst of fates, though it is undoubtedly hard on one's old acquaintances, the ones most likely to remember us in our vigor and grieve over our ruins."

Dying from the top down, as you once put it.

"Precisely."

Dying from the outside in is probably preferable, but not without its own forms of distress. You and I would make an odd couple were we to meet today, even more comical a pair than we made in Philadelphia four decades ago. Unlike you, I can still see well enough to consult my books and my papers, and despite a painfully stiff wrist I am able to manage a pen, but my hearing has grown so dull that I doubt if even the most loyal secretary or patient grandchild could put up with reading to me. I can still ride eight or ten miles in a day, if I need to visit my infant university and consult with builders, but walking only a few yards from my front steps into my garden produces the most profound fatigue, and I have to rest before attempting to return. You would have to abandon me to my fate on one of your three-mile rambles.

Thomson's plight seems uniquely deplorable and yet fascinating at the same time. It would have appealed to his own philosophical nature had he remained in command of his faculties.

Lately I have become engrossed by the most extraordinary book sent me by my Paris agents, a study of the brain by a young French anatomist who has found a way to keep pigeons and rabbits alive while he opens their skulls, excises portions of nerve tissue, and studies the effects on their behavior. The brains of these creatures loosely resemble our own, having each a stem that ascends from the spine into the base of the cranial cavity, passing through a midbrain or a cerebellum and ending at the cerebral hemispheres. A bottom to top arrangement in which the sections are clearly distinct and must, so he believes, play equally distinct roles in the animal's being.

To pierce the brain stem is instant death. Its sole function seems to be that of a channel conveying nervous energy to and from the skull's interior chambers, a portal to an otherwise inaccessible citadel. Removing the cerebellum deprives the animal of any control over its limbs, though it remains otherwise alert and active. The cerebral tissues appear to contain all the secrets of consciousness. Deprived of these closely coiled bodies, a pigeon will starve on a mound of grain. A rabbit shows no interest in nibbling a fresh green leaf. The creatures have complete command of their bodily mechanisms but can direct them to no purpose, not even to bare survival.

"From your description I conclude that these are not the sort of investigations that a reasonable person would attempt on an eagle or a bear, and when your young Frenchman is done with his specimens at least he can eat them, rather than the other way around."

That advantage occurred to me as well, but my main interest in the work lies in its potential to fix the mind in a precise physical location, to seat it firmly in matter and so dispense with the ridiculous fictions of spiritualism.

"Farewell to your *manes* then."

It has served its purpose. The cerebral hemispheres, however, still have many secrets to reveal. They rest on their subordinate structures like a bust on a pedestal or a flower on its stem. Thomson's mind is clearly a wilted blossom, one that his industrious bees must already have stripped of its vital nectar. He appears to have experienced some partial dissection, severing many links to his memory but without depriving him of speech or reason. His intelligence is not extinguished, however feeble its remaining glimmers of light might be. An eye-draught of his mental wanderings conducted by a skilled anatomist might even be able to detect the deepest chambers of his soul, the refuge where his few remaining stories reside and where he has hidden himself away until the engines of existence fail.

I am beginning to feel more than a few qualms about comparing him to a cabbage. He is, as you have implied, a poignant ruin.

> "The two of us have gone over much of this ground before. My impatience with metaphysics is as great as your own, but on matters of spirit I am an agnostic. You, on the other hand, are reluctant to lay your head upon the soft pillow of ignorance."

I am reluctant to concede that the grasp of our senses has a limit beyond which we can never hope to inquire. The young Frenchman I mentioned is a protégé of Cuvier, with many years of startling work ahead of him. He may yet find the locus of the mind in creatures more complex than pigeons or rabbits, perhaps even in ourselves. In time he may uncover the first fountain of consciousness and of reason. The fontanelle in the skull of an infant was once thought to be the window that linked a newborn child to its celestial origins. As it closed, so did the mysterious channel that gave us access to the ground of our being. These new experiments may reopen the window. When that day comes, we can dispense with the many brutal idiocies of revelation. Even the Incarnation myth will become as archaic as the tale of Athena bursting from the head of Zeus. It will be a crucial stage in the emancipatory dream.

> "When that stage arrives, you may count me among those who will miss the figure of Wisdom as a warrior queen, born from the brain's laboring womb. I much prefer that fable to the ludicrous proposition

> that the Sovereign Intelligence of the Universe chose to descend into living flesh in order to be spit upon by Pharisees. But having achieved the crucial stage you mention, what will follow?"

Some account of universal time and space that our senses can apprehend as clearly as we do the rotation of the globe or the phases of the seasons. Is the cosmos self-existent from all eternity as the atheists like to claim, or does it have an antecedent cause that we can actually describe in language that does not drift into jargon? Can we arrive at a deeper understanding of our passions, our reason, or our dreams? I do not share the Spaniard's conviction that we are condemned to a nightmare life, victimized by the basest elements in our nature, that our intelligence is doomed to sleep forever, subject to the feeble reassurances of priestly intervention, sacramental superstition, or the cruel restraints of tyranny.

Such expedients are suitable for an ignorant age perhaps, but ours is passing beyond such limits. Knowledge is steadily encroaching on the shadows; uncertainty is giving way to certainty. Even now I am convinced that I know many, many things, and yet none more surely in these latter days than that I love you with all my heart and have done so for the past fifty years and more.

> "The operations of the heart, I take it, are not among the brutal idiocies you mean to purge. No emancipatory dream would have been worth the price."

No. I entirely agree.

Now that you speak of unacceptable prices, however, I am reminded that a Richmond printer has had the effrontery to write me for permission to assemble our recent letters and publish the whole. My hand must have been recognized in the post offices. I hope none of the envelopes reaching you show signs of tampering.

A dialogue between the last of the Argonauts, the printer calls our belated correspondence, and hints at the profits my daughter might expect to enjoy.

I intend to burn my copies, along with those from you that seem to me unsuitable for the public eye, particularly those that describe our breadcrumb excursion. Let the pictures we have been discussing speak for themselves whenever a reader of my book should happen to light upon them and begin to puzzle over their significance. The bedside memorandum will remain behind to start the whole machine in motion, but I expect it, too, will soon disappear as casual scraps of paper generally do, slowly disintegrating in the bottom of a letter box until only a yellow flake or two remain.

Appendix: Four Drawings

One

The monument that the bedside memorandum describes was never built to the memorandum's specifications. By the time a variation on the gravestone was put in place on its wooded slope, the author of the unsigned description had been dead for seven years and his house sold to help pay some of the debts of the estate.

The coarse stone that the memorandum called for made inscription difficult. The results, on the cubic die, probably proved unsatisfactory from the first moment that the stone was incised and have only deteriorated over time, though the stonecutters apparently tried to address the challenges that the stubborn material presented by enlarging the letters and dividing the dates of birth and death into three lines rather than a symmetrical two. The more elaborate wording of the shipping label was even less easily accommodated on the rough surface of the obelisk. Rather than attempt to do so, the heirs arranged for a single engraved tablet of Vermont marble containing the entire epitaph to be fixed on one face of the stone only, not on all four faces as the author of the memorandum intended. No one seems to have given any thought to adding the Anacreontic lines to the grave.

The heirs did scrupulously adhere to the wording of the shipping label and to the dimensions that its author stipulated for the marker's two pieces, a six-foot obelisk on a three-foot cubic base, each of a single stone. Visitors almost immediately began chipping off souvenirs and loosening the marble tablet to such a degree that the heirs were soon forced to remove it for safekeeping. Over the course of fifty years, according to one newspaper account, the damaged markers were replaced three times and its two original sections stored away for eventual donation to the first public university founded west of the Mississippi in lands that the memorandum's author had arranged for the nation to purchase but that he had not mentioned in his epitaph. The stones now stand on a campus in Columbia, Missouri, elevated on a small plinth, with a replica of the marble tablet that contains the shipping label affixed to one face of the obelisk. The original tablet is too fragile for outdoor display. The edges of the obelisk have weathered to the point where it might be said to resemble an old loaf of bread.

In time, Congress appropriated funds for a new grave marker twice the size of the original in smooth granite with a carefully beveled edge on the cubic base that supports the obelisk. The whole structure is so massive that a team of ten horses was necessary in order to haul it up the mountain and set it in place. The shipping label still appears on only one face of the stone. The burial plot remains the property of the family and is protected by a high metal fence. The entry gate is ornamented with a gilded laurel wreath and a coat of arms, the design of which appears to be spurious.

Two

The large engraved map of Virginia and its immediate neighbors, including parts of two New States that were gradually taking shape to the west and north, has appeared in no modern text of the *Notes on the State of Virginia*. A full-scale reproduction was slipped into the back cover of a recent collection of the author's writings, issued as part of an ambitious, multi-volume series of the nation's literary classics. The map, however, seems to have been too expensive to include in all but the first edition of that volume. Readers who order a copy today in the hope of exploring Piss Pot Island will find no carefully folded onionskin guide tucked into a tidy pocket of its back cover.

Nor will they find included among the generous collection of letters and papers that the modern editor has selected a complete version of the book that the map was originally meant to accompany. Like many recent editions of the *Notes*, this one omits all four appendices, the first three of which accompanied the book's first commercial printing. The final appendix contained a vindication of its author's character as well as a defense of his text conveyed by an extraordinary archive of voices from a lost wilderness that he had gone to some pains to recover. It is the second longest section of the entire book, richer and more dramatic in nature than many a contemporary television serial or popular movie. Even today the order of documents originally assembled for a pamphlet that appeared near the end of the eighteenth century reads like a modernist play.

The first important edition of the book to be published in the twentieth century, scrupulously annotated and containing all four appendices, included a reproduction of the engraved map as a frontispiece illustration reduced to less than one-sixth of its original size and divided over two pages. Even with the aid of a magnifying glass most of the lettering is unreadable. Digital versions of the original map prepared by Peter Jefferson and Joshua Frye in the middle of the eighteenth century are readily available online, but it is more difficult to locate images that reproduce the changes and additions made by Peter Jefferson's son when he was preparing an updated copy for the London engravers who were helping to prepare the first printing of *Notes on the State of Virginia* meant for general circulation. The most affordable paperback version still in print today contains no portion of the map, though it is otherwise a complete text.

Until some new publisher emerges who is willing to reproduce the book's first or second edition in its entirety, or who is willing to maintain a digital link to a complete image of the map for the use of curious readers, a balloon voyage down the Shenandoah Valley toward Poplar Forest, Madison's Cave, and the Natural Bridge will not be feasible.

Three

The eye-draught of Madison's Cave that appears in *Notes on the State of Virginia* would seem to be the first attempt to map any of the dozens of caverns that are scattered up and down the limestone ridges of the eastern seaboard. Many of these have become modern tourist attractions, equipped with lights, railings, and wooden walkways to make the experience of visiting them as convenient, informative, and profitable as possible.

The two individuals who made the eye-draught, however, were only the first to bother mapping the cave's passageways, not the first to explore them. A very young George Washington was among the cave's earliest visitors and, apparently, left his name on its walls sometime before 1750. He in turn must have heard of the cave's existence from local people who may have made a habit of visiting it in part to collect the bat guano that accumulated on its floor, a substance rich in potassium nitrate or nitre, as it was known at the time, an essential ingredient in the manufacture of gunpowder as well as one of several naturally occurring salts that could be used to cure meat. Turgot and Lavoisier experimented with large-scale chemical processes for converting guano, manure, and other organic materials into quantities of black powder capable of supplying the needs of the French Revolution. Madison's Cave was, for many years, a chemical mine as well as a natural curiosity.

At present the cave is privately owned and sealed with a steel gate to preserve its delicate limestone formations, to safeguard the occasional bit of historically meaningful graffiti, and to protect the habitat of a creature known as the Madison's Cave Isopod, an endangered crustacean, blind, colorless, and not much bigger than a grain of rice, that was first discovered in the cave's freshwater pools. It is now found in a handful of similar underground habitats along the Allegheny ridge. Heavy metal effluent, primarily mercury, deposited in the Shenandoah River by a defunct factory may ultimately contaminate the two quiet basins that lie at the bottom of the cave.

Four

The Baker's Bottom sketch, when it makes its way into modern editions of the book at all, is usually printed in reoriented form, turned ninety degrees to the east in order to place north at the top of the page where most readers and editors expect it to be.

The maker of the original tracing arranged for it to be printed in rotated form three times, in two successive editions of a pamphlet entitled "Relative to the Murder of Logan's Family" that appeared in 1800 and, a few months later, in the final appendix to his book. Nineteenth-century editions of *Notes on the State of Virginia* sometimes maintain the rotated position but print the image backward. At least one modern editor acknowledged correcting what he considered an authorial oversight in the map's appearance. The only other widely available edition of the book for classroom use prints the reoriented map without comment. No editor has ventured to add red ink to the tracing, though that suggestion occurs only in a handful of letters written near the end of the author's life, all of which now appear to be lost.

About the Author

Douglas Anderson grew up in southern Ohio, attended Oberlin College, and did graduate work in American literature at the University of Virginia. He spent nearly forty years in college teaching, most of them at the University of Georgia where he retired in 2017 as the Sterling-Goodman Professor of English. He has written a number of critical studies including *Pictures of Ascent in the Fiction of Edgar Allan Poe* (Palgrave, 2009), *The Unfinished Life of Benjamin Franklin* (Johns Hopkins, 2012), and *The Introspective Art of Mark Twain* (Bloomsbury, 2017). In 2000 he received a Guggenheim Fellowship to support the completion of *William Bradford's Books* (Johns Hopkins, 2003). He and his wife currently reside in Portland, Oregon where he has spent the last few years experimenting with writing novels.